The Woman of Stencils and other stories

MARIANNE PRICE

ISBN: 979-8694795692

To my husband, Bill.

Contents

The Meat Cleaver

'So, she's back after all these years, the one you called the Meat Cleaver.'

'And what would *you* call her, Nikos?' I looked across at him, almost knowing full well what he would say.

'I'm not going to tell you, not even in Greek,' he replied, as he helped me lay out the last of the blue and white checked tablecloths.

It was already still quite early when we finished setting out the tables in the taverna ready for the long day ahead. We hadn't yet set eyes on her, but news had a way of travelling fast on our island. It was Georgina, who had first told me, her husband who worked on one of the ferries that regularly went back and forth from Kos to my home town on the island of Kalymnos, had spotted her making the journey over. She was much older of course, but Yannis was never one to forget a face. Then Andreas, one of the former sponge divers, had heard from his mother who had got wind of her arrival from another son, whose job entailed checking passports at the airport. So, in fact we were all ready and waiting, though not one of us would be looking forward to seeing her. She was a woman that would best be described as being notorious, but of course Nikos most definitely could think of a word that would be more suitable. And although what she did to me all those years ago was initially callous and despicable, causing such a painful awakening, it provoked my decisiveness to totally change the course of the path that I was on at the time. So, in some strange way I felt indebted to her for what she set out to do and achieved. Without her intervention I would have been the one who would have been classed the loser.

It was more than eight years ago when I first came to this island, and to this day I will never forget my first sight of Pothia, as it came into view from the overnight ferry that I was travelling on. Such a long journey with endless delays and hold ups that neither Gavin nor I ever thought we were going to get there this side of Christmas. It was the first time that either of us had been to Greece, having gone to quite a few other places in Europe before. However, for this trip we had decided that we wanted a holiday that was more leisurely and laid back, and an island in the Dodecanese more than appealed. I can recall how the packed ferry started to stir as the port became more apparent, and although at the time I was feeling rather exhausted, I managed to make my way to the top deck with the other passengers who like myself didn't want to miss out on the early morning sunrise that had started to show itself. I left Gavin still sleeping on one of the inside decks and hauled myself up the step ladder to the top open deck, in time to watch the daylight start breaking over the rooftops behind the harbour. Like the many tiers of a wedding cake, the houses were stacked high on top of one another behind the port itself, drifting purposefully away from the medley of streets and reaching far up the rising mountains framing the town behind. During my stay, I was to learn of the other houses, the ones in the town that held surprising gardens, all hidden away from view. Each one like a planted sanctuary, leading out from the backs of graceful houses, being havens that only a certain few would get the privilege to see, or as in my case be allowed to spend precious time in.

The docking of the vessel commenced and the erratic scramble for cases, personal possessions and small children swiftly got underway. Gavin roused himself and together we made our way with the dozens of other travellers towards the front of the ferry ready to embark. Although early by our standards, the port and its surrounding streets were already alive with people. Shutters were starting to be raised and goods were already being unloaded. Large cartons from the ferry were taken off and piled erratically onto whatever means of transport was available, ready for delivering to whosoever might be waiting for them somewhere on the island.

An old dust covered taxi was waiting to take us to our hotel, the Apollo, in the tourist resort of Massouri Beach on the North-West of the island. Gavin and I had both equally looked forward to the two weeks holiday and, as the taxi speedily drove us away from the harbour, I felt sure that in coming to this island we had made the right decision. The sights of undisturbed wildflowers in passing fields, idle grazing donkeys and elderly forthright women in black; all this was the start of my initiation to Kalymnos. I breathed precious air as it came in through my open window, absorbing the unfamiliar sweet smells and welcoming breeze, moving my head even closer to let it penetrate through every strand of my loose hair, cooling me down to the roots as it did so. Rapidly our driver drove his car speedily on along the coast road ever westwards towards our destination. Then an imposing sight immediately came into view. Rising proudly out of the blue water and, seeming only a short distance from the shore, was the overwhelming vision of the volcanic island of Telendos, it's dramatic position and command of all the surrounding scenery never once failing to move an onlooker.

Massouri, although a small holiday resort, was so much quieter than it is today, just the one street with a clutch of small tavernas, plus the odd bar dotted along the road. Our unassuming hotel was of the basic Greek variety, with whitewashed walls and crisp, newly ironed, cooling, cotton bed sheets. It was located favourably, and within a couple of days Gavin and I had slowed our pace down and started to really appreciate our surroundings. I remember at the time how it had all seemed so very comfortable, just like our relationship.

By the Wednesday of the first week we had eaten in most of the tavernas, either for lunch or evening meal, but mainly we had frequented one that really appealed. It was while we had just finished our meal one evening that I first noticed her; for her gaze was most certainly directed over at the pair of us.

Though unbeknown to me, she had already seen us the day that we had arrived. Not fully Mediterranean I thought as I returned her gaze, possibly some mix of European in her blood, although she did have the distinctive features of a woman from the region, which gave her quite an unusual facial appearance. Because of this uniqueness, she more than stood out from the crowd and this was something that I was to later learn amongst other things, that she totally relished. From the look of things she didn't wear her dress, it wore her, wrapping around her fine contours as if it had been skilfully designed with her in mind, which was totally at odds with the simple restaurant and the casual clothes of most of the diners.

I decided that she'd just thought we were familiar, a couple she might once have come across sometime before and gave her no more thought as we left for the short walk back to the Apollo. How wrong I was to imagine it was something that simple.

The next day we made the short boat journey over to the island of Telendos, finding delight in its clear waters and safe bathing in an easily reached secluded sheltered bay. We had got there early after deciding to take the first boat out and found a really good spot looking towards Massouri Beach across the short strip of sea. And as the morning went by only a handful of people made their way over to the bay from the subsequent ferryboats. I caught sight of them as they approached, relieved that they were few in numbers, not wanting such a peaceful spot to be overrun. But as I got up to yet again go into the sea for another cooling swim, I could see someone coming down the dirt path who was instantly recognisable. It was the woman from the taverna the night before. She was alone and carried with her belongings a rolled-up sun umbrella giving the impression that she had come prepared for the day. As I began my stroke, I couldn't help but notice where she had decided on making her pitch on the beach. It was a good spot, a small patch of untouched sand by the start of some rocks, I had chosen it first myself, but Gavin insisted on being that much closer to the water's edge. Once she had laid down her towel, set out her things and assembled her umbrella she was totally self-contained. She didn't don the ubiquitous bikini, but then making a statement with individualism needs more than resorting to the obvious. Like the dress the previous night, her swimsuit showed impeccable taste in her choice. The overall colour of the one piece was the deepest of pinks, like the petals of a vibrant fuchsia, and of a classic design that most definitely spoke the word expensive. She didn't swim at first, taking her time I noticed before she went in, and then when she did she swam a fair distance, much farther than I, or even Gavin for that matter would have dared venture.

When she had finished her swim and got out of the water again, I saw her looking intensely over at us, just as she had done the previous night. It was not the look of admiration like I had displayed for her choice of swimming costume, it seemed to be something far removed from that. Almost mocking I thought, and it made me feel slightly uneasy.

A leisurely day always slips idly by, especially when confronted with nothing to do except swim and laze in a peaceful setting. So, when finally our senses indicated it was the time to leave, with much reluctance we packed away our things and started to walk away from the bay.

'What's that glistening over there by those rocks,' said Gavin, pointing in the direction of the spot where the woman from the taverna had been lying.

Shielding my eyes from the forbidding sun, I followed the direction of Gavin's outstretched finger, and saw something silvery reflecting in the light. With eager schoolboy relish he hurried over to investigate, before bending down and picking up what he had seen. I watched as he turned his discovery over before hurrying back to show me. His long, almost aristocratic fingers opened out gracefully in front of me displaying his bounty. It was a silver compact, shaped like a seashell, very exquisite with fine curved edges clasped perfectly together like a clam, and of course quite obvious to whom it belonged.

'It's very beautiful,' I said, looking down at it in the palm of Gavin's hand, which he had outstretched, indicating to me to take it. The metal had an unusually cold feel to the touch as I took it from him, looking closely at the craftsmanship in the design. I had no desire to open it, imagining that it most probably contained a sweet smelling and costly, pressed powder intended for a complexion much darker than mine. My curiosity was to how someone could be so lax in forgetting such a lovely looking item as this.

When we had returned to our hotel, Gavin gave a good description of the mystery woman to the receptionist who immediately knew to whom he was referring.

'Katrina Brown is her name,' said the girl on reception, before telling us exactly where she lived, an apartment block directly behind the taverna where she had first been so visible.

I volunteered to be the one to return the compact, leaving Gavin to deal with the towels and wet swimwear back in our room.

The earlier uneasiness that I had felt that morning started to return, as I crossed the street trying to avoid the impatient cars as I made my way along towards the apartments. It was a very discreet and cooling block in its appearance, only three stories high set back a reasonable distance from the road. Masses of well-tended red geraniums all set out in neat groupings lined the outside wall giving the overall impression of orderliness. I scanned the names on the slips of sun-scorched paper alongside the buzzers by the entry-phone. Third one up and written by hand was her name. Pressing the accompanying small square plastic button, I heard it ring for quite a while before it was answered. The sound of a quick Greek sentence flummoxed me, as at the time I had no knowledge whatsoever of the language. Embarrassingly I apologized that I didn't understand.

'Don't concern yourself, I speak English'. Her voice spoke reassuringly.

I then went on to explain that I had an item, which my boyfriend had found on the beach at Telendos and believed it to be hers.

'Come up,' she replied, and hearing the lingering buzz of the entry system I hastily made my way inside the building.

When I reached the top floor, I saw that she was not as I had expected waiting there to meet me, she had instead left her front door slightly ajar. I knocked tentatively before hearing a low toned voice beckoning for me to come through. What greeted me was not the sort of place that I might have imagined someone who gave off such style to the outside world would chose for a home. I recall that it was rather tired looking, plus there was more than a hint of ostentatiousness about the place, having gilded wall mirrors and marble occasional tables set out amongst the once cream furnishings. There were also far too many trinkets and ornaments crammed together in a glass cased mahogany unit giving me the impression of the owner being something of a collector.

Katrina Brown was sitting in what I assumed to be her favourite spot in the room, to the left of one of the sofas, which like the unit was also overflowing, but in this case with plumped up embroidered cushions. Its saving grace was that it commanded the best position as it allowed her to look out through a pair of sliding glass doors to a small balcony with sea views directly out across to Telendos. She was wearing some sort of floor-length robe, similar to a kaftan, with a pulled-in tie belt around its middle. Although an impressive floral pattern in shades of turquoise and red, it was not everything that it seemed, for it too looked quite aged and showed discreet signs that it had even undergone some minor repair at some time. However it did suit her, though its style was so very different to the impeccable dress I had previously seen her wear in the taverna, and I thought that it must have had some sentimental significance for it to be retained and for her to wear it.

'Don't tell me,' she said as she put a hand up to stop me from speaking. 'It's my compact isn't it?' she added, before indicating for me to sit down alongside her, 'I knew the moment that I had got back that it was lost'.

I took it from my holdall and handed it over to her.

'You must think I was very stupid to leave something like this on a beach.'

I half smiled not really knowing what she expected me to say.

'Would you care for a drink, some coffee?' she enquired of me.

Although I had the words ready to reply in polite refusal, I decided instead to change my mind and accept a glass of lemonade, mainly because I had not had a drink for quite a while which had left my throat feeling quite parched. After she gave it to me, she mentioned she'd noticed both Gavin and myself when we had first arrived, which made me wonder how we could have been so memorable. I recall that I must have been in her company for possibly half an hour or so, and although we had a conversation of sorts, she didn't once divulge anything significant about herself. As I left the building, I felt cheated in some way, as if I had given out more during that brief interlude than I had received. Like a highly experienced surgeon skilfully extracting only the essential, she had left me feeling partially robbed and vulnerable from allowing myself to become so exposed.

A sense of deflation set in, which made me hardly feel like talking about my encounter when I returned to an eagerly awaiting Gavin. I tried to play down the meeting with Katrina and hoped that my mood would clear. But the afternoon's events seemed to cloud my mind so much that even after our meal that evening when Gavin insisted on a nightcap over at the bar of the taverna we were in, I was adamant that I didn't want to go. A mindless argument started up between us, transpiring in him obstinately going to the bar alone, and with me defiantly setting off back to the hotel. Manoeuvring my way through pairs of idling couples all seeming oblivious to the fact that they were strolling directly into me, I was relieved when I caught sight of the

Apollo. Though just before I made my way up the steps to go inside, I caught a glimpse of what appeared to be someone observing me from the opposite street corner. However due to the headlights from the passing vehicles, it was impossible to distinguish their features. Straining my eyes amidst the glare, I waited impatiently for the traffic to ease. But when the lull came and I eventually managed to see over to the other corner, the moment had passed and the solitary figure had moved on.

Convincing myself that Gavin would be back within a short while, I got into bed and although restless at first due to the sounds of the street below, finally I slept. Although it was not the best of sleeps, when I awoke the next morning I realised that I hadn't heard or been disturbed by his return the previous night. It was while he was in the shower that I realised just how long he must have been gone. For as I turned my head on the pillow, I smelt the warm scent of perfumed jasmine, not quite faded from where his head had been. As distinctive as the silver-shelled compact, it identified its owner by leaving such a memorable signature.

An expected and wearisome batch of lies and insulting explanations followed, trying to prevent me from my actions. Fortunately, as I had hastily dressed and mostly packed while he was still in the bathroom, there weren't too many of Gavin's empty words to endure. Somehow I managed to keep my feelings under control, and just before leaving made it clear that on no account did I want him to come after me.

Once down at reception I asked the receptionist to ring for a taxi.

'Where are you going to go?' she enquired, her knowing eyes realising what had just taken place.

'I haven't a clue. Do *you* have any suggestions?'

'Let me make a phone call,' she said lifting the receiver. I waited patiently while the receptionist spoke in Greek to someone on the other end of the phone, and then finally clicked the phone back on its receiver before starting to write sometime down on a memo pad.

I stood patiently on the opal coloured marble floor, eager to find out where fate might be landing me.

'My cousin Georgina will be happy to take you for the rest of your stay,' she said tearing off the memo paper and handing it to me.

I took the piece of paper and looked at it. Below her name was an address in Pothia.

'Is OK?'

I nodded, with a smile full of appreciation whilst she rang for a taxi. Within minutes it seemed both I and my suitcase were being packed off to somewhere totally unanticipated. At least Gavin had had the decency to do as I'd asked and not come down after me I thought, as I was sped away from the resort back along the coast road and the sea that only a week ago had seemed so enticing.

Once in Pothia the taxi started to weave its way back behind the port itself, into the start of the residential district, carefully edging through the busy streets before arriving at Georgina's house. There was a deception to be found here, but not thankfully of the human kind. It was the house itself, for its secret was that behind it hid a remarkable garden that proudly lay in wait ready for my discovery.

'You are welcome to use the house as a home,' said Georgina showing me round.

'You're very kind, I really don't know what to say,' I told her.

'It's the least I could do, hearing your situation. Do not worry you are amongst friends here.'

I looked at the unpretentious woman who had agreed to take me in and felt overwhelmed. She told me that Yannis, her husband, worked for the ferry service between the islands so she said she would enjoy my being there. If and when I wanted, I could tell that she would be a listening ear.

After the events that had happened, I found the garden was the best place for me to sit reading and listening to the pretty yellow finches that were sighted above my head on one of the house's ornate, wrought-iron-worked balconies. It was comforting to be with the family and Georgina's two young boys were especially a delight. In fact, I didn't once miss the resort where I had previously been, for now I was living like an adopted family member and quickly found that I fitted in with natural ease.

But each night before sleeping, everything that I had been avoiding came back into my head. I couldn't block it out, it seemed that it had to be dealt with.

'Can I ask you something?' I said one morning to Georgina after she had returned from taking the boys to school.

'Let's sit in the garden, it's quite fresh at this time,' she said sensing that I was possibly going to bring up the inevitable.

'Katrina Brown, do you know her?' I asked.

'Fortunately not personally, but of her reputation,' she paused, raising an eyebrow, 'of that I know plenty.' And she did, in fact like many of the Greek women on Kalymnos, with each one of them all having their own versions of her story.

Georgina told me that Katrina was the daughter of a local woman from Massouri, and an English businessman, hence her surname. Her father had come over to the island long before the early days of tourism and had married Katrina's mother when she was very young. It had been a whirlwind courtship, which at the time was unheard of especially as he was a foreigner. But because he was financially very comfortable, proving that he could provide for their daughter, Katrina's grandparents allowed the marriage to go ahead. Katrina grew up in England, with her summers spent in and around Massouri, with the family giving the impression of being a happy one. But no one was fooled, because on a small island nothing stays hidden for very long. Katrina's father very early on in the marriage showed his true colours, of that of a womaniser. Her mother's decision to ignore the situation was noted by her young daughter, who decided that one day she herself would do something so despicable that it would finally bring any such similar woman to their senses.

Thereby her actions to come between certain couples, splitting them apart like a meat cleaver became the talk of the island.

'And the men were always English,' I added almost instinctively, looking over at Georgina when she had finished telling me the story.

'Of course,' she replied.

I could see now that Katrina Brown's actions were not so straightforward as they first appeared to be. To simply entice for thoughtless pleasure and destroy a solid relationship was not her style at all. I recalled her watchful eyes that night in the taverna, when she had gazed so intently over at Gavin and I. As a couple we had seemed so at one with one another. But if all that was true, then how come it was possible that Katrina could so easily slice us in two? There had been a willing participant in the shape of Gavin, just as I expected there had been with all the other Englishmen whom she had enticed away from apparently watertight relationships. So in fact she had done me the greatest favour by her actions that night in Massouri, causing me to look deeply beyond the delusion of my relationship with an easily diverted man.

***

'Do you want some coffee?' Nikos spoke the words in Greek bringing me back to my present surroundings.

I nodded my head in agreement and sat down at one of the tables. A slight breeze blew under each of the chequered tablecloths. I looked across the pavement at the few passers-by, and it was then that I saw her. She was certainly much older and dressed very similar to the way she had always done, but somewhere along the line I knew instinctively that she had lost her edge. Like an improbable missionary on a lone quest the time for conclusion had now come. I stared intently at Katrina, the woman whose actions had led me miraculously to be the one who had attained lasting happiness.

A chair beside me moved. Nikos, Georgina's older brother, my husband of almost seven years had returned with my fresh coffee, placing it thoughtfully in front of me before sitting down. I thanked him in Greek and slowly stirred the cup. As I looked up and over in Katrina's direction, I realised that she had disappeared. Like that night all those years before when she had slipped back into the shadows on her way to seek out her prey. Though now she had no more appetite that needed satisfying, no old scores to settle, for the game she had played so skilfully and for so long had finally lost its appeal.

The Chinese Bookend

For as long as I can remember there was only ever one bookend on the shelf in our living room. I was as used to seeing it there, as I was to seeing the callipers on my Uncle Henry's legs. It was something that I'd never given any thought to, except of acceptance.

I continued to tear off pieces of newspaper and wrap up more glasses and carefully pack them one on top of the other in the tea chest in our living room. Moving was such a bind especially for a thirteen-year-old schoolgirl, who would much rather have been rehearsing her lines for her Drama School monologue. The smile on the face of the Chinese bookend seemed to be wider than ever. I never thought it odd that there was only the one, and in actual fact I was rather glad, as he always seemed to be rather an evil-looking character, or at least that was the way it seemed to me, a highly imaginative, only child.

The bookend was a representation of a short, vastly overweight, semi-naked man covered only by a loincloth. There was no hair on the top of his head, and his screwed-up, laughing face had a permanent, wide grin similar to that of the laughing policeman most seaside towns had in an arcade at the end of the pier. It was an ornament made out of china and it was clear it had been meticulously painted by a skilled hand. Though to me there was nothing attractive or pleasing about it whatsoever. There was also none like it around in the bric-a-brac shops where we lived which hinted that it had been an authentic piece of oriental art. Where it had come from or how we had acquired it, up to this moment, I didn't have any idea whatsoever.

'How are you getting on?' said my mother. 'Why do we have to have so *many* glasses?'—I answered her question with my question, neither of which received a reply. 'Fancy a cuppa tea?' she said looking over at me. 'I'll make us one,' she added. Cockney families can hold conversations with many unanswered questions, though strange as it may seem to an outside observer, they can communicate what they are saying to the person they are talking to and the question invariably gets answered without vocalized speech. Call it being on the same wavelength if you like.

A few minutes later my mother returned from making the tea and I paused from the task in hand. My tea was hot and refreshing at the same time, copper in colour and thick enough to stand a teaspoon up in as my father would say. My mother took out a cigarette from a packet, snapped the cork tip off its end and threw it in the ashtray.

'I really wish you wouldn't do that,' I said with irritation and flashed her a look of distaste.

'What?' she said, 'this,' gesturing at the broken cigarette end with her finger, 'or smoke?'

'Both,' I said.

'I know you don't like me smoking,' she said stating the obvious.

'You can say that again!' I replied sarcastically.

'Well, when I was expecting you, the doctors encouraged it to calm the nerves,' she added.

'Well, if you must smoke,' I was backing down now, as I knew I was upsetting her and didn't want to do that, 'why do you have to break the end off, that's what I find so revolting.'

'It's a better smoke,' she added, 'and anyway, they don't make this brand without the filter, it only comes in a filter tip, simple as that,' she answered in a matter-of-fact way.

'Are we taking *him*?' my head gestured towards the mantelpiece as I changed the subject, my eyes glancing over at the figure on the ledge.

'The Chinese Bookend?' my mother replied, 'I've not made up my mind,' she paused and hesitated slightly with her words, 'I've not yet decided if he's coming or going this time.'

This time! It sounded as if moving house was something we did as a matter of course, as some people might change their underwear or a woman the colour of her hair. My mother inhaled deeply on her cigarette, I watched as she exhaled the smoke through her mouth, full, red-rouged lips puckered and pursed and rounded. Lastly faint trickles of slightly translucent smoke descended out of her nostrils. The ritual of her smoking a cigarette, which although I disapproved of, transfixed me as it gave her a slight appearance of a Hollywood vamp. She would be a character I would imitate to a greater or lesser degree in various guises in my chosen career of an actress many years later.

The blue-grey eyes of my mother, one with a mark, a minute fleck of brown, which was the result of an engineering accident from her factory days during the war, a spark of hot metal burning and scarring its rim, now stared hard at the object.

'You've never bothered to ask me why there's only the one,' she said turning round, 'surprising really, you with your inquisitive mind.'

'I know, I suppose I just got used to him. So, are you going to tell me the reason?' I replied, giving her my full attention. I sat back in my chair knowing from her body language she knew she had a captive audience and also that I was going to hear a story, but a story that I could never have dreamed up or imagined with that vivid imagination of mine because it was all hers. It was just as much as the topic of the story the Chinese bookend was hers, and now the tale of this rather obscure object that would never adorn a shelf as one of a pair, was about to unfold.

'Before the war it was,' she began, '1938 to be precise, and I was working mostly nights in a factory. I used to get by with very little sleep in those days, we all did, and me, well, I loved going out ballroom dancing, it was my passion. I could hardly get enough of it. I danced till I felt I would almost drop, it was my main enjoyment and hobby. There was a reason for it as well. You see I'd been engaged to be married to a chap I'd known from when we were kids, Bill his name was, Bill Matthews, old Wheezy Anna they used to call him, it became his nickname because of his asthma. He used to make wheezing noises because of the tightness in his chest and his difficulty in breathing, poor love. Well Bill and I both had motorbikes, his was a Norton and mine an Aerial Square Four, beautiful machines both of them, for their time that is. Anyway, 10 days before our wedding day, we were out on Bill's bike, the Norton, and as we were approaching Bruce Grove along the High Road, an old woman suddenly stepped out in the middle of the road in front of the bike. Bill braked hard but, unfortunately, it was too late. He died instantly from the head-on collision and the old lady died shortly afterwards from multiple injuries. I received only a few minor cuts and bruises, amazing really considering the impact.' My mother paused for a brief moment before speaking again.

'Time heals all things, or so they say, and after a few months of coming to terms with the accident I gradually started to get back to normal. I went out dancing again as much as I could, mostly down the Tottenham Royal, that was my haunt, it was a great dance hall then, it really was; lively, vibrant, with big bands playing mostly, and very quickly I started to find a new crowd to hang out with. And in that crowd was a bloke called Harry, Harry the Eel they called him.' Why the eel?' I asked. 'Eels are slippery things aren't they? You've seen me prepare them for stewing,' she replied.

'Yes, and don't they wriggle!' I replied.

'Harry was a slippery character all right,' she told me continuing with her story, 'there was no mistaking, but at the time I thought he was fun and great to be around. He worked as a bookie's runner, taking bets, and always dressed like a bit of a spiv now I come to think of it, but he was a good dancer, a very good dancer, in fact, and he was what I needed, someone to make me feel alive again. Three months later on a Friday evening I was standing with Harry on the doorstep of your Nan's house, and in my hand was that Chinese Bookend.' She raised her eyes up to the shelf. 'We'd been out with some friends Elsie and Bert for a drink, and they had given us a present. It was quite badly wrapped and started to partially open so it was easy to distinguish the bookends. We each took out one of them and I remarked how unusual they were, saying that it was possible that Elsie, my friend, had come by them from her father who worked on cargo ships that went out to the Far East. Then suddenly without any warning Harry turned his face away said he couldn't go through with it and was off like a shot.

'Go through with what?' I asked quite puzzled. Bright for my age I certainly was, there was no question of that, but this was even a bit too much for my understanding.

'We were due to get married at Tottenham Registry office the next morning,' my mother said dryly.

'He'd been two timing me all along, the bugger, and gone off with a widow he'd met down Walthamstow dog track. Freda was her name, and she'd been left a corner shop and a few bob, so it seems Harry thought she had the edge on me. Apparently he left it right up to the night before our supposed wedding before he did a runner, because of something to do with the timing of Freda's dead husband's will, and him playing us off, one against the other. Though he got a bit more than he bargained for as a few weeks after he married her he came home to find a house full of kids that she'd not mentioned before, having had them stay over at her sister's till she'd 'got her man' so to speak. And she was nothing like me in the looks department,' added my mother proudly tossing back her long, thick, auburn hair. 'Freda was never anything to write home about. Didn't stick with her either by all accounts. Heard he wasn't so good with handling the cash and cleared off when things got tough. Rumour had it he was bragging that he had bigger fish to fry', she informed me.

'So, are we taking the bookend with us then?' I asked rather apprehensively.

'I've told you I haven't yet decided,' my mother replied as she helped herself to another cigarette.

We only moved twice after that, all four of us if you counted the bookend, and the last time was to a sprawling housing estate up by Bruce Castle Park, right behind the cemetery, which suited my parents as naturally it was nice and quiet.

My own life started to change very rapidly as my theatre career began to take off, and my parents' life changed though at a much slower pace as they settled into their retirement. My father was still involved with the local Labour party as he had always been, and my mother, as she had always been, remained my best friend and confidante. She was still an attractive woman even in her sixties, and I used to laugh when bus conductors did a double check at her bus pass, as she certainly never looked her age.

'Oh, damn and blast,' said my mother somewhat agitated one Saturday morning as we were weaving our way through the tangle of stalls in Walthamstow market. She stopped walking and started to rummage through her handbag. 'I think I've gone and left my lighter at home'.

'Here take these,' said a voice suddenly from someone nearby. Looking over I could see a heavily veined hand had thrust a box of matches straight out in front of her. I then noticed that the hand belonged to a worn-out looking man, someone whose clothes had seen better days and he had a tray attached to a strap around his neck which had boxes of matches in it.

My mother gave an emotionless glance at the face of the person offering her the matches before getting her cigarettes out of her handbag, removing one which she put carefully in her mouth, and then taking the box from the outstretched hand she picked out a match and struck it violently on the side of the box to light the waiting cigarette that she had placed between her lips. Throwing the match to the ground she pocketed the box before walking swiftly away. I stood where I was for a moment unable to fathom out why she had just done that before having to quicken my pace to catch up with her in the busy market. When we were eventually side-by-side again I turned to her and said, 'A box of matches isn't much money to you or me, but they might be to someone selling them for a living in the street.'

'Oh yes, and with far less profit than from selling them from behind the counter of a corner shop,' she replied, before tossing her cigarette into the gutter.

The Card

Pauline's sadness started not that long after the warming glow she had felt when first looking at the picture on the front of the card she was holding. She always bought her cards and stationery from the same familiar shop which was run by an elderly woman and her now middle-aged son. It was a little gem of a place, unchanged by the passage of time in the sense that it had not succumbed to the tacky and tasteless that was now to be found in the usual chain store type card shops, no furry cartoon animals or false sentiment and definitely no piped music. Its cosy character reflected and shone in the type of cards that were to be found in the faded, wooden racks lining the walls all around the shop. A paper emporium was what it was, a glorious place to while away fifteen minutes or so in the surrounds of beautifully crafted and versed cards that fitted every occasion. Not once had Pauline in the ten years that she had lived in the town failed to find something suitable, until today when she would come out empty handed.

Her fingers held the card almost reverently as if it were of great importance. It would have been ideal she thought to herself, the words were just as she liked them to be, simple and straightforward, nothing more. More was for leaving to the imagination, for those who had one. Colin had an imagination, which is why this card, although on the face of it was a perfect fit for the occasion of his forthcoming birthday, was not the one. Something in the content of the picture was the reason. It was the picture itself, which evoked such strong feelings in Pauline. She looked hard at the image displayed there, a reproduction of a painting of a street scene she hadn't come across before. That was another one of the good things about this shop, the owners managed somehow to find cards just that little bit different, having an eye and feel for quality and originality from the supplier whose company produced greeting cards for them. The card in question, had all the elements that would entice someone to buy it, a cheery vision of a time gone by, of a small picture -book high street in an imaginary town with attractive women in hats and upright men in trilbies walking along a pavement carrying their shopping. But there was more to the picture than just the street. On one corner was its main focus, a welcoming little place called 'Ivy's Cafe'. It was so well executed that it drew you in through its windows, so you could see the customers packed tightly in enjoying their snacks, with the faint steam from a tea urn gently billowing in the background. Pauline lingered with the card as she lovingly remembered how her mother once worked as a waitress in a place similar to this when Pauline was a young teenager. She had been a very popular waitress with the customers and used to say, if she had the money, she'd open up a place of her own and call it by her name Ivy. But of course, like most dreams it stayed that way, with no possibility of being fulfilled. Money for the most part of her life had been hard to come by. Hard to earn, but not hard to spend, which was something Pauline had inherited. This was an annoyance at times to Colin her husband, just as it had been to her father in his day with her mother.

Pauline put the card back in the rack from where it had come from. If only it had said something like 'Lily's' or 'Ada's' or even 'Brenda's Cafe' she would have bought it. But the name of her mother, although Colin had nothing against Ivy, having never met the woman as she had passed away years ago before they had married, was not really appropriate, it evoked Pauline's past, something that he had not been a part of, something he wouldn't understand. No, the card was too personal, and she would have to find something else that had some relevance to them or held some interest for her husband. In haste she picked up a card with a kingfisher on. Colin was a keen fisherman, so the card would be topical. No, she wouldn't rush it, she thought to herself and put the card down. She could always come back another day; there was plenty of time before his birthday, six weeks in fact.

A week went by before she went into the card shop again, this time for some new stationery to write a letter to send to her oldest friend who now lived in New England. The urge to look again at the picture on the rejected birthday card was overwhelmingly strong, and she found her fingers flicking through cards and envelopes on the rack where it had previously been, but it wasn't there any more, it had been sold. However, Pauline found some stationery that lifted her spirits, the borders of the writing paper having delicate drawings of pastel sweet peas entwined round the edges. Janet, her friend in Boston, would surely love those she thought, they would remind her of the ones that used to grow in her garden when she lived nearby. The middle-aged man behind the counter took the money from her, and carefully put the stationery in a paper bag that was covered with patterns of subtle peach rose petals.

'Thank you Leonard,' she said calling him by his first name, and added as she took the envelope from him, 'too lovely to give away, you'll have to start charging for these as well.'

Leonard smiled at her little repartee. 'Thank you, Mrs Atkinson, as I was only saying to mother the other day, it's customers like you that make it all worthwhile.'

Pauline walked back to her car and thought about Leonard. He seemed happy enough, devoted to his widowed mother Alice, who had owned and run the card shop for over fifty years. She was a dear old soul, hardly seen very much these last few weeks, age and arthritis finally creeping up and taking their toll. Leonard seemed to manage well enough and appeared outwardly at any rate to be as happy as a sandboy. He'd never married, never had the opportunity he once told Pauline, what you've never had you never miss he'd told her, and besides, he had added, if what he had seen of it from behind the confines of his counter was anything to go by, he was rather relieved that he'd stayed a bachelor.

The car engine started up straight away, and Pauline headed for home.

***

'I hope I'm not expected to go to that wine bar you're so fond of,' the voice on the telephone said accusatorily.

Pauline mustered up all the patience she could before she gave her reply.

'No, Florence, we aren't going anywhere this year, Colin said he'd prefer to stay at home.'

'Well I suppose that's one thing to be thankful for. So you'll be round to collect me at the usual time, 6 o' clock, you know that I don't like to eat too late.' she said before continuing, 'Lays on my stomach, stops me from getting to sleep, don't know how you 'youngsters' do it, eating halfway into the night. Wouldn't do for me at all.'

No, I don't suppose it would Pauline thought as she listened to Florence chattering on for a few minutes more. It wasn't that she was a difficult woman, not by a long chalk, a little trying from time to time like old people can get, yes that had to be admitted, no, the fact of the matter was that she and Pauline didn't quite hit it off. Call it that old chestnut the mother and daughter-in-law syndrome. Pauline replaced the receiver and thought about what she would cook for Colin's birthday meal tonight. And then she remembered, remembered that she had forgotten to get Colin his birthday card. Somehow these last few weeks had gone by with a flash, no that was no excuse she told herself, it was that she had just plain forgot.

She left what she was doing and rushed off down to the card shop. Its window was decked out as usual with a wonderful array of assorted cards to entice the passers-by into its Aladdin's Cave-like den. Pauline's experienced eyes took pleasure in the well-dressed display, which Leonard's fingers had so immaculately arranged. She then entered the shop to select Colin's card. Once again, her eyes started to search for the card that she had seen from previous weeks ago, the one with 'Ivy's Cafe' in the picture on the front. Almost obsessively she hunted through the racks, again to no avail, her failure at not finding the card leaving her with a feeling of empty hunger.

A suitable card for Colin showed itself, almost popping up from the rack which had the word 'husband' written above it, in a delicate hand on a sticky label. It was a safe bet, safe option of a card with a countryside scene, nothing that would stir or inflate the imagination, and simply sincere in its sentiment.

The birthday itself was a low-key affair just Pauline, Colin and Florence sitting round the dining table eating a meal of roast chicken followed by trifle, which was home made by Pauline. She had bought Colin a new sweater, stylish with an Italian label, one that he had admired in Barton's window more than once in passing, which delighted him no end. The card was a different matter, it was received with quiet thanks and a slight smile that accompanied Colin's usual acceptance of minor gifts of no real importance. Colin's mother's card on the other hand was a different kettle of fish altogether. It was in a word, perfect. Her choice of card every year for her son was always spot on, impeccable. The card this year depicted a riverbank with a swan and her cygnets sitting on it, printed from a painting beautifully done by a local animal artist, and Colin was delighted with it. As always Florence showered Colin with plenty of gifts, and like the appropriate card, they were enthusiastically accepted.

Pauline was relieved when Colin took Florence home, though this year's birthday hadn't gone too badly all things considered. The reminiscences of birthdays gone by when Colin was a little lad and Florence had baked him a cake with coloured candles on it, and the party games with the other children who lived in their street, yes, Pauline had heard the same story many times before and sat in unendurable silence the other side of the room while the two of them, mother and son, had shared stories of events that had long since passed but still remained fresh and alive for both of them.

Within two weeks the memory of that birthday was wiped clean away. Another, much stronger by far, had replaced and cemented itself, the funeral of Florence, who had died just three days after Colin's birthday, of a massive coronary. Naturally, the house was flooded with cards. Cards of condolence filled with appropriate words and written verse were pushed through the door and left lying on the mat in the porch. It was remarkable in the number of people who sent their sympathy, and well-meaning thoughts. Pauline thought the card shop must have supplied most of the cards as they looked like the sort that would have come from there with their quality and appropriateness.

After the initial shock, Colin seemed to cope very well. Pauline did think that because he had been extremely fond of his mother and been his mother's favourite in the family, that he would react rather differently. However, surprisingly he managed to function pretty much as normal, save for the occasions that Pauline found him standing in the conservatory, looking out through the windows down the long garden, his opalescent eyes staring out at nothing at all.

The small ground floor flat that Florence had lived in was shortly put on the market. It was expected to sell rather quickly, as it was fairly modern, well-equipped and in a pleasant area of the town. Florence had kept it neat and tidy, preferring to have only a few cherished ornaments on display, carefully avoiding anything becoming cluttered.

'I think that we should go round and sort out the things in the flat,' said Colin one evening looking over at Pauline.

'Well, I suppose it has to be done sometime,' Pauline replied, 'Though are you sure you want to do it so soon?' she added, 'We could always leave it a bit longer, you've only just put the place up for sale.'

'No,' Colin sounded adamant, 'I think it should be done now, get it over with, easier that way.'

So, the following Sunday morning equipped with a few cardboard boxes and black plastic bin liners, they let themselves in to Florence's flat, and started the arduous process of clearing out her things. They decided to make a start in the bedroom, and Pauline sensitively waited for Colin to make the first move, with the removal of clothes that were hanging up in the wardrobe that strained at the seams from the weight of its contents. She herself carefully collected the assorted bottles of hand cream and suchlike that were on the walnut-veneer dressing table, her movements reflecting in its three mirrors, one main and two smaller ones.

'There's something down here,' Colin indicated towards the back of the wardrobe 'Can't see what it is.' He leant down and pulled out a gift-wrapped package, lying next to a pair of dated, silver, evening shoes, and matching bag.

'It's got your name on it, Pauline,' he added passing it over to her.

The little gift tag had solved the clue.

'Oh, it's for my birthday,' she said with surprise. 'But that's not till July, five months away,' she remarked as she sat down at the dressing table and started to feel the package with her curious fingers.

'I want to open it,' she added, her voice gleeful, like an inquisitive child.

'Go ahead, it's your present.' Colin replied.

She hastily ripped the paper and in doing so a note written on crisp, white vellum floated down onto the dressing table.

Opening it she read the few chosen lines written in Florence's neat hand.

'My dearest daughter-in-law, I hope you like what I have done for your birthday. Cherish it, along with your memories.

Fondest wishes

Florence.'

Inside lilac, patterned gift paper, the present exposed itself from within delicate tissue paper that had been placed around it for extra protection. It was a framed picture of the street scene and Ivy's Cafe with its billowing urn. In fact, it was the very same card that Pauline had rejected, but which Florence had bought and then carefully cut and slotted into a complementing, mahogany-coloured, wooden frame.

Pauline's piercing scream misted her reflection as she fell forward onto the dressing table, and as she reached out the waiting mirrors wrapped themselves around her like a comforting cloak.

Ripe Cherries

I had been going to the Flamenco class for many weeks before we spoke, although noticing her I had not had any reason to strike up a conversation, and also because afterwards she somehow seemed to disappear as quickly as she had come into the hall, like a will-o-the-wisp. I did know her name, hearing it in passing from the lips of the tutor as she spoke directly to her regarding the payment for some dance shoes. Laura, the name itself echoed across the polished parquet flooring, suiting her perfectly, a match for the image she gave off, one of a free-spirited creature.

My reasons for joining the class were not driven by an overriding urge to learn to dance Flamenco, they stemmed more from a curiosity of trying to learn something a touch out of the ordinary, instead of the proverbial pottery, badminton or beer making that inevitably seemed to dominate the evening classes in the area, and which were not, by any stretch of the imagination, my scene. The class itself was a motley collection of a few women and only two men, making a grand total of eleven. Fortunately, our enthusiasm compensated for what we all lacked in numbers and natural ability. That was to be found in the spellbinding routines of Sophia, our tutor, and the excellent guitar playing of her husband Miguel. I, for my part, knew from the off that I would never in a month of Sundays make a dancer, Flamenco or otherwise. I had deluded myself thinking that anything might be possible, but on seeing Sophia the artist at work, and trying desperately to follow her steps and hand movements, I knew that, although I was remembering some of them, the dance itself was beyond me. It was this impossibility that led me into conversation with Laura.

'Well, that's me finished with Flamenco, I'm sorry to say.' I said speaking to no one in particular as I took off my shoes at the end of a lesson.

'Surely not, you seemed to be doing so well.' Laura's voice at the end of the changing room was the one that took the trouble to reply. Although there was softness to her tone, for overall she was quietly spoken, because of her projection and impeccable diction, I could hear every word.

'Oh really, you could have fooled me,' I replied and then added, 'look, thanks for the compliment, but I don't think its worth my while continuing.'

Laura moved towards me buttoning up her almost ankle-length, long, black coat as she did so.

'You enjoy it here don't you?' she said almost inquisitively.

I was slightly struck off balance by the somewhat change of direction in her few words and before I could reply Laura had spoken to me again.

'I'm going for a drink, would you like to join me?'

I was surprised at her sudden show of friendliness.

'Yes, thanks for the invite,' I answered and then added, 'I won't be in the way, I mean if you're meeting friends or someone.'

'I was going on my own,' she informed me.

I looked at Laura, she was the type of woman who, if this was London or any one of our large cities, it wouldn't come as a surprise to see her walking into a bar or pub alone, but in this place, this sleepy backwater of a small town, her actions seemed somehow out of step with what was considered the norm. Later when I got to know her better, I realized that for her it was standard practice, and I accepted it as being part of her quirkiness, like many things I was to learn about her, making Laura all the more endearing as our friendship prospered and grew.

'He's nice, isn't he?' Laura said in a low whisper as the barman turned away to serve another customer at the bar. She pursed her lips slightly on the ridge of the wineglass and took a small sip.

‘I can’t say I’d really noticed.’

‘I’m only passing comment,’ she said putting her glass down on the bar. ‘I hope that you don’t think for a moment that I was meaning anything by it,’ she added, sounding almost quite prim and indignant.

‘I didn’t believe so, it’s just that men, good-looking or otherwise, aren’t down on my agenda at present.’

‘Is that why you started going to Flamenco?’

‘It was something to do, something I thought would be interesting,’ I told her.

Laura looked as if she wanted me to continue.

‘What do they say, oh yes you should keep yourself busy, occupy your mind, or so all the best-selling paperbacks on the subject keep telling me, the ones with titles like, ‘Being dumped is the most positive thing that can happen’, or ‘I’m so in charge of my life, I don’t need a man to screw it up.’ I picked up my glass and took a large swig.

She smiled and laughed, a tickling chuckle of a sound and as my own laughter joined her, I felt that at long last I’d found someone in this dead-end town that I’d be able to relate to.

In talking, we found a commonality in that we had both come to the area not through choice or employment, but because of the wrong man, and in Laura’s case because of the wrong husband.

‘So, will you continue with the class?’ Laura said as we made our way out into the street about an hour later.

‘I feel I should throw the towel in, it’s not fair on Sophia, she’s so patient and encouraging, but realistically I’m no dancer,’ I told her.

‘You’re too hard on yourself, you really are. You were getting the steps and doing quite well, and besides no one expects any of us to be anything like professional Flamenco dancers,’ she replied as we continued walking. ‘Just treat it for the enjoyment, like I do.’

‘Ah, but at least you’ve got the rhythm as well, that’s more than can be said for the rest of us.’

'It must have rubbed off from my husband.' her voice was distant, 'Now he *really* had rhythm.'

'Was he a dancer then?' I asked with interest.

'No, he was a gas fitter, but he had a fabulous physique and it was all black, very black. His rhythm came from his soul and oozed out from every pore of his beautiful shiny body. That's what first attracted me to him.' She paused and faced me. 'Look I have to go. I hope I'll see you next week at the class.' And then after quickly checking for any traffic she rushed across the road, her self-evident sense of freedom flying high, and soon she disappeared from my view, vanishing into the darkness.

If it hadn't been for that interlude with Laura, and her kind comments, I might have stopped going to the Flamenco class. In which case I would have undoubtedly missed the fun times that she had touched on which we most certainly had as the course progressed, as well as the sense of achievement, albeit small, in the sense of acquiring something of the art of the dance, from mastering a few simple steps and hand gestures, and mainly from the realization that it was doing more for my self-worth than I had ever imagined possible.

As well as Flamenco, the class started to develop a keen interest in Spain and the Spanish way of life. This came about shortly after a superb Spanish meal at Sophia and Miguel's just before the Christmas break, pleasantly rounded off with guitar playing by Miguel which filled us all with early Christmas cheer, and then the following January shortly after we all returned from the break, George, one of the two guys in the class, organized a trip to see Antonio Vargas and his Jaleo dancers in London. By coincidence, the local film club started a season of Spanish films, and then a local travel company offered a trip to Seville at a price that sounded extremely tempting. Sophia put up a notice board for the class with the title 'All things Spanish,' so that anything interesting could be listed, and we then added our names if we intended to go along. Because the meal at Sophia's and Miguel's was such a great success, Sophia suggested that she and her husband would be willing for it to become a regular monthly event, taking place on the last Friday of every month, with everyone chipping in something to cover the food and drink. I remember how I always gave Laura a lift there and back again on these evenings, and even now my memory is still fresh with the vision of her oddly waiting for me propped up against a street lamp along from where she lived, a book in her hand, and her eyes screwed up scouring the printed words as she forced herself to read in the dim light.

'It's bad for your eyes,' I said one Friday as she got into my car, feeling at ease with our friendship, knowing full well words of concern would not be mistaken for interference.

'Yes, I suppose it is, but what can I do?' she shrugged her shoulders as she gave me her reply.

'You could let me come round and ring your bell for a start,' I said as I drove off, heading out in the direction of Sophia and Miguel's.

'Oh no, I couldn't let you do that,' she said firmly.

'Laura, I know you don't want me to see where you're living, but what's wrong with me ringing the bell, I don't have to come in, you could just follow me straight out, it would save you waiting outside in all weathers.'

'It's really thoughtful of you, but I don't mind really, and I'm never waiting there that long,' she answered sensing that she had hurt my feelings. 'Don't take it personally,' she added, 'it's not you, I'm like this with everyone. I won't have anyone call for me. I always meet people somewhere else. Actually, you're the only person who I let come anywhere near my flat.'

'I'm honoured then,' I replied, somewhat sarcastically.

'I told you before that I only have a couple of shoe-box-size rooms and I'm not very tidy so I wouldn't want anyone to see them, even if that was the only reason,' she said, before continuing.

'Since I left Nathan, my husband, I decided that I would keep something of myself back, and that's what I've been proud of doing. So, each time I close my door, I exclude the world and retreat into that small space that I call my home, to be able to do and be whatever I want.'

So, Laura's private life, the one she guarded and kept separate from me and everyone else helped her remain amongst those whose souls are uncaptured, who are forever the eternal free spirits amongst us.

I continued driving until Sophia and Miguel's road came into view and then managed to park directly outside their house. That evening there were only a small handful of us there, as George and three of the others of the class had decided to take up the travel agents offer of a long weekend in Seville. It was still very enjoyable, starting with Sophia passing round tapas, while Miguel served the drinks. After the meal and a few glasses of oaky, red Rioja, we listened while Miguel once again played his guitar, his fingers quickly picking the strings like a web-spinning spider, transfixing us all as he made beautiful, relaxing sounds.

Laura had that evening mingled with her usual ease, talking to everyone in turn, plus the fact that she was a good listener tended to make her even more popular. She was a real people person, with the ability to draw a conversation out of even the most hard-nosed clams of the class. Also, she was fast becoming the best dancer amongst us. Of course, being Laura, and full of modesty she was embarrassed when it was mentioned. Even Sophia had told her she had an unusual natural ability for someone who was not from a background rooted in the dance itself.

She talked quite freely on the way back that evening, almost elated, telling me about plans she had regarding her job. Although she had worked for a long time at the local hospital as a physiotherapist, she was thinking of leaving and going into a private practice. I listened intently, not knowing whether or not any of this was likely to come about, not because I was a confirmed cynic by nature, but because as the months of our friendship went by, I heard so many different schemes and ideas from Laura's lips, without any one of them actually getting started.

As I stopped the car next to the now familiar lamp post, she blurted something out of the blue to me.

'I saw my husband today,' she told me, before adding something very strange, 'he still has a taste for ripe cherries.'

I thought this remark more than odd, even for Laura, and didn't respond.

'Oh, didn't I ever tell you about his delights?' she spoke like a woman from the past with her strange turn of phraseology. I shook my head, not knowing what to reply.

'He used to tell me about them, how delicious they were especially the ones he enjoyed the most.'

'Well, they can be rather moreish, especially when they're very ripe.' I said, trying to enter into this unusual conversation.

'You don't understand!' she replied and started to laugh at me, like people do when a child has made a wrong remark. It was only then that the penny dropped.

'Mental cruelty can be a terrible thing,' I told her.

'Yes, it can,' Laura said opening her bag to get out her door key. 'I suppose I ought to do something about getting a divorce. Seeing him by chance today made me realize that. I'd just left it, like a drawer that you know you really ought to sort out but keep putting off.'

She opened the door of the car and I watched her as she carefully stepped outside onto the lamp-lit pavement.

'I have to tell you, I won't be coming to Flamenco next week, I've so much else to do,' she said, and added, 'I'll try to give you a ring sometime soon.'

But she didn't. Neither did she come back to the class again. Naturally, I wondered why, but knowing of the unspoken boundaries within our friendship, I felt that I was at liberty to do nothing that would encroach on her wish for silence.

I continued to go to the Flamenco class, finding pleasure from those heady evenings, and from the sense of achievement that accompanied my sometimes successful attempts at winning over a few more of the steps of the dance itself. I thought of Laura often, and how it was she who had initially encouraged me to continue just for the sheer enjoyment. It wasn't until nearly two years later before I saw her again. I'll always remember the weather that day, it was pepper hot, and the start of a very fine summer that was not to be wasted. I had gone to the town market extra early that Saturday, so as I could savour the perfectly picked produce on the stalls before making my selection, and also to avoid the cramping crowds.

At first, I wasn't sure that it was Laura, her hair having been cut differently to the way she had worn it before, was now a twenties-style bob. It more than suited her and accentuated her long narrow neck, the paleness of which contrasted with the tanned-up bodies of the stallholders as she weaved in and out from underneath their canopy- covered stalls. But it was only when she stopped to take some coins from her purse in payment for some apples, that I truly recognized her, just from that one movement. It was exactly the same one that she had used when getting her door key out of her bag when I used to give her a lift home. And then suddenly it was she who spotted me, and literally only a matter of seconds before she came over towards me. I can still visualize seeing her now, looking so delicate yet somewhat contained with a glowing sense of her inner strength, her cotton-printed dress wafting gently in the faint hint of breeze, as she approached me.

'It's so very nice to see you again,' she said in that strange way of hers that was directly out of another time.

'How are you, Laura?' I answered.

'Me? Oh, I'm fine, things couldn't be better.'

She smiled all the while as her eyes surveyed me, looking closely into my face. I imagined it was to find something that was detectable only to her.

'Do you still dance the Flamenco? I remember I once told you not to give up.'

So, she had remembered something of our friendship I thought.

Yes, I still go, and I find it very worthwhile for more than one reason.' I looked down indicating my left hand. 'I'm married now, to someone I met at the class,' adding, 'He might not be Spanish, but he's a mean Flamenco dancer.'

We both laughed at the humour in my words, and I felt like the clock had been turned backwards closing the gap of the last two years.

'I'm pleased for you,' she said finally.

It was only then that I noticed them, directly in front of us on the stall, amongst the mountains of fruit. Ripe cherries, handfuls of them, reddened and darkened almost burgundy black ready to be consumed.

'Oh, look, aren't they tempting, I think I'll buy some,' I said as I moved forward to make a purchase.

'They don't appeal to my palette,' Laura said disdainfully. 'Now the ones that I prefer are actually much sweeter than those. Like over there for example.' She turned and used her eyes to indicate somewhere beyond us.

I followed her gaze into the distance scanning the stalls, but I could only see blurred images of green and orange fruit.

'I have to go now,' she said suddenly sounding as if she had forgotten something. 'I'm glad you've found your happy ending.'

'And you Laura, what have you found?'

She leaned towards me and spoke almost in a whisper. 'Someone quite delicious.'

And then she moved away, quickly going off down the long line of stalls before pausing next to someone underneath a canopy. There I saw her link arms and watched as the two of them walked out into the glare of the bright sunlight, till there was only a vague outline of their two cotton dresses.

Cat No 46

'You do realise that he will have to go?' said my husband, his voice firm and his mind obviously made up.

'Yes, I know, it's not working out at all with her.'

We had both hoped that it would and waited patiently for them to hit it off. That they did, but not in the way that we had envisaged. No gentleness or cuddling up together and definitely no bonding. Their way of hitting it off was of the hitting kind, a scaled- down version of a match between Mike Tyson and a lesser opponent, with left and right hooks being thrown at every conceivable opportunity, and fur flying everywhere.

We had gone to the rescue centre to get a replacement for our old tomcat, that due to illness had been put to sleep a month before, and getting another male cat seemed the perfect solution. Frankie, or Frankie Boy as we had nicknamed him, was the friendliest cat in the centre at the time. Apparently, he had been found walking the streets of London, a rough sleeper of the feline world. Surprisingly, he was not at all in bad shape, and except for a couple of scars on his ears he looked quite healthy. Plus, he was absolutely huge, well massive really, and picking him up was like lifting a giant orange and white woolly plaything.

But after we had returned Frankie to the rescue centre, we both wondered if in fact we had done the right thing, and by the end of the week I knew that I had to get him back. But having signed him over it wasn't going to be easy. It seemed that getting him out again would be the equivalent of springing someone from Wormwood Scrubs. I made endless tearful phone calls, and then a friend said that she would take our little female cat Koko, so that the problem would be solved. Finally after thinking about it for a while the supervisor of the centre relented and I rushed off before it was due to open, to wait outside its closed gates like a mother desperate to be reunited with a lost child.

'You'll have to find him yourself,' said an assistant curtly, as she left me alone in a vast corridor of caged creatures. Frantically I rushed up and down, peering into wire cages containing cats of every conceivable colour and size, and then I saw him, in a small cage with a ticket that said in a plain hand 'Cat No 46.'

Three months have passed since that day and he is now a permanent fixture in our lives. As for Koko, well she didn't go to my friend at all, we decided to give it another go and remarkably they have worked it out between themselves in their own catlike way. They will never be 'an item,' but they have a toleration and respect for each other, just as much as we now do for them.

Vanishing Act

George put down his paperhanging brush and stood back to survey his work. Yes, he thought to himself, it was coming along quite nicely and before the end of the afternoon he was confident he would be finished with the wallpapering. It was a lovely kitchen of a well-proportioned size and he was sure that it would look revitalised from his painstaking efforts. He never cut corners with his work though he knew plenty in the game who did. Although now retired he was still every inch a professional. He took out his soft, brown leather tobacco pouch from a pocket in his white overalls and started to make himself a thin cigarette carefully rolling a few golden strands of loose Virginia tobacco into the tissue-like paper held between his fingers. He walked over to the window in front of the sink unit and, as he took his self-imposed mid-morning break, he looked out at the fine view of the well-tended garden and its small orchard of apples. Rose would be envious when he got home and described it all to her. She had heard about the house many times from George's brother but that was all, she never expected in a month of Sundays that she would ever be invited round for a visit. George, of course, was being allowed round because he was a skilled painter and decorator. It was the one thing her husband always came in handy for especially now when his brother's son Alan had decided to get his house done up.

George thought he should go outside to smoke his cigarette and made off in the direction of the orchard. Loads of windfalls were scattered around underneath the trees making a fine carpet of bruised fruit for the worms. No doubt, later on in the afternoon, Alan's wife Gillian would collect and fill up her apron with damaged apples and then offer them to George to take home to Rose. This thought George did not relish. Gillian was known (according to family gossip) for trying to palm off the old windfalls on to all and sundry.

No one could understand why as it wasn't as if they didn't have more than enough apples for themselves there being apparently twenty-six fruit trees in the garden which yielded enormous quantities every year. He finished his cigarette and then walked back to the house skirting around the small pond that Alan designed and had had contractors put in the summer before last. Ready to continue with his wallpapering he returned to the job in hand.

George worked steadily on only stopping for a half-an-hour's break at midday to eat his cheese and pickle sandwich that Rose had prepared for him earlier that morning. He'd brought his own tea in a large flask and was sitting on the kitchen step just finishing his lunch when Alan unexpectedly appeared having come back home from work for some case papers that he now needed.

'Hello, Uncle George, what are you doing sitting here?' asked his nephew from inside the kitchen, 'Hasn't Gillian offered you any lunch?' he added.

'It's alright, lad, I always bring me own,' George replied turning round.

'Well, the least I can do is to make you a fresh cup of tea. I'm sure you wouldn't say no to that,' said Alan as he picked up the kettle and proceeded to fill it with water. He'd turned into a fine man and a good solicitor, by all accounts, though to his uncle he would always be referred to as a lad.

'Is Gillian not home then, Uncle?' Alan enquired as he started to make the tea.

'Said she had some shopping to do and went out about 10 o'clock time', George answered.

'I expect she's met up with someone,' said Alan, 'I'm afraid it's only bags, Uncle George,' he added apologetically, 'but we do have a teapot.'

George grinned, no he didn't suppose Gillian went in for things like loose tea, she was more the convenience type of housewife, she even told him so herself. She liked meals that had quickness in their preparation, cooking and consuming. Gillian wasn't that interested in food, to her it was only fuel for the body, like petrol to a car. No, she was more interested in stimulating her mind, not her taste buds. She did some part-time working from home, something to do with consultancy for a number of firms. George didn't know what consultancy Gillian did do, having no idea what it meant and not wanting to show his ignorance he had kept quiet on the subject. He did though know about one type of consultant and that was the one he and Rose had seen prior to her having her gall bladder removed. He understood about that one alright.

As the two men drank their tea their talk was mostly about business with Alan telling George his plans for the future and George reminiscing about forgotten dreams from his now fading past.

'So why didn't you set up on your own, Uncle?' asked Alan.

'Oh, I thought about it many times but putting it into practice,' the old man paused, 'well, that's a whole different ball game. You see times were different then and there was always the problem of money. You needed a good bit to set yourself up and to keep a family going. No, lad, in the end I decided it wasn't for me. I was one of the luckier ones of my generation and managed to keep going, what with working as one of Charlie Moore's gang of decorators and sometimes picking up the odd job on the side. So, I can't grumble.' He placed the empty teacup down in the sink. 'Glad to see you got to run your own business though, you've done us all proud, especially your father.'

'Well, it's not been easy, not by a long chalk, it's tough getting to where you want to get and even tougher staying there.' Some of the strain that Alan normally hid so well was beginning to show. 'I'm planning on expanding this year and I'll be taking on another partner. It's about time that I started to off load some of the work,' he added before continuing, 'and now that I'm more established it makes good business sense.'

He reached over to the hand-stitched cuff of the jacket of his tailor-made suit, pulling it back slightly, 'Gosh, is that the time already, I'd better get my skates on if I'm to get to my next appointment.' He made his way over towards the kitchen door.

'I suppose you'll be gone when I get back, Uncle George.' he said looking rather forlorn.

'Yes, I expect to be away by four, it should all be done by then.'

'Well, we must definitely arrange for you and Aunt Rose to come over and have a meal sometime soon. I'll talk to Gillian about dates and let you know.'

When Alan had left, George thought about the prospect of having a sit-down meal in Alan's dining room, the one that he had finished redecorating only last week. No, he thought to himself he couldn't imagine it ever coming off, him and Rose sitting down to eat with Alan and Gillian, even with Alan's good intentions he imagined it would just be all talk nothing more, because Gillian, although appearing pleasant enough on the surface, wouldn't allow it. The thought of spending an evening in her posh dining room entertaining the brother of Alan's father, no, he knew she wouldn't go in for that. She only tolerated having George's brother Sid and his wife May over on rare occasions, like birthdays, anniversaries and the like. George picked up another roll of wallpaper and started to unravel it and proceeded to do the last bit of wallpapering on the last wall. Then as he had predicted by four o clock he was finished.

Gillian, who had returned earlier in the afternoon, was most impressed with the redecoration of the kitchen and after paying him gave George not one but two bags full of windfalls claiming Rose would really appreciate having them adding once the bad bits were chopped out there would really be quite a lot of apples.

Alan and Gillian lived in the most desirable part of Chingford whereas George and Rose lived in a not so desirable part of Hackney where they had lived all their lives.

When George returned home, he found his daughter Yvonne was there having popped round earlier to see her parents. She lived in Stoke Newington, the area that had become very trendy quite a few years before and it was an ideal location as it was not that far to drive to her parents.

'Hello, Dad, I've just put the phone down on Alan, he asked if you could ring him back on his office number when you got in.'

'Wonder what that's all about?' George answered, racking his brains not being about to think what it could be. It wasn't about payment as it had been agreed that Gillian would pay him.

'Maybe you left something behind,' said Rose coming into the hallway, 'It won't be the first time if it is.'

George went out to the hall and picked up the telephone and dialled the number that Yvonne had written down on the pad next to the phone.

'Whatever's the matter, Dad?' said Yvonne when she saw the look on her father's face as he came into the living room. 'Here, sit down, you look like you've just had a shock.'

George hardly heard what was being said to him, it was like a far-off, distant voice and very hollow. He let Yvonne help him into his chair and after a while he began to speak and told them what Alan had said to him over the phone.

'Gillian's engagement ring has gone missing,' he said.

'Well, they can't suspect you,' said Yvonne rather indignantly.

'I bet it's that Gillian, she's probably put it down somewhere and can't remember where,' said Rose trying her best to lighten the situation.

'Oh no, apparently she knows where she left it,' George said looking over at his wife.

'And where might that be?' answered Rose.

'In the kitchen by the side of the sink.'

The highly charged air in the room had become frozen as each of them in turn looked at one another, searching for clues to an answer to was to become a mystery, the disappearance of the engagement ring.

'Go and check your tool bag and then turn out your pockets,' ordered Rose flinging her hands up in a gesture of annoyance at the situation. 'Just in case somehow it's ended up in your things,' she added. George did as he was told and more besides. After checking his tools and turning out his pockets he was made to go into the back bedroom and strip off completely while Rose went through his clothes with a fine tooth comb turning every piece inside out not once but twice over, all to no avail.

George, in his mind, knew he was thought of as an underdog to someone like Gillian, who would regard him as a menial servant and therefore not beyond doubt. Alan, of course, had naturally thought there was some logical explanation to the matter and said to his uncle that he thought Gillian was mistaken about where she had put the ring in the first place and it had simply been mislaid. He had rung to find out if George had noticed it lying around somewhere else in the kitchen. George told his nephew he had never seen hide nor hair of the ring all the time he was decorating the kitchen. Only once had he seen the ring and that was just a quick flash of it many years ago at Alan and Gillian's engagement party. Alan felt confident that very soon the ring would be found. However, after George put down the phone he felt uneasy and could imagine the behind-the-back family gossip and unseen finger pointing. In his heart of hearts, he knew that he would feel much easier once the vanished ring had reappeared.

It didn't help matters either when Rose came home the following afternoon and told George how she had run into his brother Sid's wife May and that she had told her the value of the engagement ring. It was worth five thousand pounds.

On Gillian's insistence a police investigation was launched, and statements taken from all parties who were there on the day of the disappearance of the ring which was, of course, just Gillian and George. But no culprit and no leads were found. The weeks gradually passed with no one hearing any news at all about the ring other than the fact Alan had put in an insurance claim for its value. All this came as second-hand news from May.

George never took on any more decorating jobs, not even for his daughter Yvonne and her husband, although they tried desperately to twist his arm hoping that, by doing so, he would manage to pull himself out of the depression that had enveloped him ever since the saga of the ring had taken place. But George was adamant he would never pick up his paperhanging brush ever again. As the months and then years went by the unsolved mystery faded in the thoughts of the rest of his family but not to George, it was always there in his mind as fresh as when it had happened. Although not having been a religious man, he started to say a small prayer to himself at night before silently sleeping for the ring to be found and relief to be his. He never set foot in Alan's house again and contact with his brother became slim, only in passing did they now speak and that was only on the off chance for neither side went out of their way to break the invisible barrier that had formed like an ice sheet between them.

The memory of the last time George ever decorated when he applied his paperhanging brush to the walls of Alan's kitchen haunted him like a tantalizing spirit. As his mind became racked with innocent persecution, his body started to respond, the outcome of which was that he started to develop a fast-growing, incurable cancer. Within a short time a hospice was arranged for George. He didn't fight the plans to go there, in fact, in some ways his mood seemed to lift as if he welcomed the outcome, and he even commented on his room remarking on how it had been skilfully decorated, admiring the careful attention to detail in the way the matching up of the paper had been done.

He didn't have long, the doctors said, possibly a week or two at the most, but told Rose and Yvonne not to worry as they were very good at relieving the body of pain with the drugs they had to hand. Plus, all the staff were dedicated and extremely kind, so George would be well looked after right up till the end. Their freely encouraged visits were plentiful and conversations without remorse took place there being no point or time to waste on painful regrets. George managed in between periods of drug-induced sleep to listen and join in with their everyday talk and as is often the case with someone who is dying, eerily he looked remarkably well.

Three days after he had been admitted Yvonne came surprisingly early one afternoon to sit by his bedside. She sat for a full hour watching her father as he lay sleeping not wanting to disturb him but longing for him to wake up, itching with an almost childlike excitability for him to open his tightly-closed eyelids and focus on her with pleasant recognition in his eyes. Eventually he stirred and reached out over towards her with a thin, wasting arm. Yvonne clasped the outstretched hand gently and held it between her two palms.

‘I have something important to tell you, Dad,’ she said, trying to slow down her speech, though the urgency to communicate her news was filled with strong emotion and the need to speak.

‘I had a telephone call at lunchtime from Alan. Gillian’s ring has been found.’

At first, she wasn’t sure how her father would respond. George looked over to his daughter with puzzlement and then stretched his head forward a fraction, clearing his throat before he replied.

‘Oh,’ he said in a voice that was now soft and quiet.

Yvonne then poured out the story that was now taking everyone by complete surprise.

Gillian had been out in the garden picking up windfalls and she noticed something glinting beside her as she was clearing the ground of the fallen fruit. There it was her once lost though not forgotten engagement ring partially covered in dirt amongst the apples more than three years after the day it had gone missing. Alan had, like his wife, been surprised and extremely pleased to know the ring had been found and when he returned from work went out to see the spot where the ring had been discovered. He was bemused as was Gillian as to how it had got there and then he heard the cackling sound of birds above his head and looking up he saw two magpies hovering above before they returned to their nest in the large imposing tree directly above his head that was fanning its branches in the breeze almost beckoning them not to delay. Gillian then gave some information that she'd not mentioned before, that there was the possibility she had made a mistake and left her engagement ring on the ledge by the window and not by the side of the sink unit at all.

'I remember now Gillian had opened the window to let in some air,' said George to his daughter, 'to clear the smell of the paint,' his mind now returning to that distressing day.

'Yes, she said she did and it must have been one of those magpies who saw it shimmering in the sun and took the ring up to their nest. But before the bird managed to get there it must have dropped it amongst the windfalls,' she added.

'Like undiscovered treasure just lying there under all those rotting apples,' said George softly looking out of the window in his room, feeling such bitterness but not towards the malevolent magpies but for his relief that was now much too late in coming.

A Good Likeness

‘Ere he really sounds like him dun he, Fay?’ Eric said across his shoulder to his colleague who was busy making the final amendments to her notes for the performance that evening.

‘What was that you said, I didn’t quite catch it?’ said the overworked and somewhat harassed Deputy Stage Manager continuing making some notes in the prompt corner, almost unaware of the young electrician’s mutterings.

‘Him over there,’ Eric pointed to the sound check that was taking place a few feet away from them on the stage.

‘I suppose he does, but then some of these tribute bands are pretty good value,’ said Fay stopping what she was doing for a second to look over at the impersonator. Eric was right this guy had the sound and resemblance even without the costume. Strange really, she thought to herself, this fad for an illusion, something that looks and sounds like the real thing. Apparently according to the crowds that were drawn to this type of entertainment, that was partly what it was all about. They seemed to revel in the delights of watching performers who were imitators of all-time legends. Fay looked at her watch. Just over an hour to go now before the start of the performance. On stage the band was now finishing its sound check. It called itself ‘Like Satin’ and was a take-off of the highly successful and talented 70s rock band ‘Bright Satin’. They, of course, were renowned, having been extremely popular at the time, filling vast stadiums around the globe with their concerts. Sales of their CD compilations of their greatest hits were always in the top twenty rock albums list. The tribute singer Fay noticed having just placed his microphone back on its stand was walking towards the wings near to where she was standing. He smiled slightly as he passed her on his way back to his dressing room. And as he did so, Fay was surprised when she noticed that he was much older than she thought he would have been, compared to the rest of the band. But as Eric had rightly noticed, he did sound very convincing; there was no getting away from that. Yes, he did look similar to Ian Stanley, even though he was a rather older version.

'How much longer are you going to keep this up for?' The voice on the end of the phone sounded agitated.

'I haven't yet decided. I'm enjoying myself too much.'

'It's ridiculous. You know it is and, if it gets out in the business, you'll be a laughing stock.'

'I don't care.'

'Ian, it's crazy. Just what are you playing at?'

'Playing myself, and loving every minute of it and, if you don't mind, I've got a show to do tonight.' And with that Ian Stanley hung up on Clive Morrison his best friend and bass guitarist from the good old days with 'Bright Satin'.

Except of course a lot of those days had never been that great, bloody hard work and petty arguments if the real truth was ever told, and all these years later they were still falling out with one another. Although, of course, from Clive's perspective he did have a point. The 'bet' that Ian had taken on by Clive after a night of rather one too many bottles of lager, daring him to go and perform as himself with a tribute band had now got seriously out of hand. Ian, whom it was well known and every so often documented by the media, had been a recluse for decades. Until now, when this irresistible challenge had shaken him out from his seclusion, and taking on his own persona, albeit a younger version, he had for the time being no intention of stopping. The tribute band, all of them sworn to the utmost secrecy, was also enjoying every minute of it. To perform with their idol, even though up close he looked old enough to be their dad, didn't matter. This was the real thing, and for the next few nights they were experiencing a rather unusual slice of rock history being made.

'It's open you can come in,' Ian said when he heard the knock on his dressing room door.

'Just checking if everything's alright,' Fay replied edging herself round the door of the artist's room.

Ian put down his brush and shook the lion-like mane of the blonde wig he was holding.

'Yeah, yeah, it's great, it's just like it used to be,' he answered, placing the elasticated front of the wig firmly against his forehead and pulling it back over his balding head sharply, before patting it down into place. Fay watched as he started to twist and twine strands of synthetic hair into cascading curls dangling down onto his shoulders.

'Sorry?' said Fay quizzically.

'I mean, err,' he stumbled for the right words to cover up his mistake, 'like when I used to sing in a pub band.'

That was truthful enough, as Ian had when he started out sung in pubs. However, this was way before he joined a line-up that eventually became 'Bright Satin', who after they were discovered, went platinum with their first album, which catapulted them all to instant stardom.

Fay nodded, acknowledging that she understood what Ian had meant.

'Well, if you're quite sure there's nothing you need, I'll get back.'

'Thanks, hope you enjoy the show,' he added, continuing to adjust the curls.

He did look rather good, she thought to herself as she closed the door behind her and made her way back along the corridor to the wings. With the thick pancake makeup and 70s costume the years would fall away under the lights up there on the stage. She made her way over to her position in the prompt corner and prepared for the start of the evening's performance. The tribute show, which had been sold out for weeks, went down a storm, and 'Like Satin', due to the overwhelming appreciation of the audience, had to do two extra encores of greatest hits before they could finally leave the stage.

'Brilliant! If you closed your eyes, Fay, you would think it was the real thing', said a somewhat over enthusiastic Eric, bouncing about in the wings to the beat of the music.

Fay didn't look up; she was too busy with the run up to the end of the show. She gave out her instructions to the flies for lowering the curtain, and then once they had been lowered, she removed the cans from over her ears and placed them on the hook by the side of the prompt desk. During the course of the evening, Fay had looked over at the band, observing parts of their performance, rather than just looking at them from a technical viewpoint. The likeness of the vocalist to a young Ian Stanley was remarkably good she thought, the wig with its cascading mass of flowing locks seeming to obscure parts of his face, therefore his age was not so obvious. And as for his voice, well that really was something else, as the sounds he could make were colossal. The rise and fall of each crescendo, the vocal pyrotechnics, they were all there. Remarkable really, thought Fay, after all these years and he can still manage to do it. She'd had a hunch that it was the legendary superstar from the moment she had come face to face with him in the stark light of the dressing room. His facial features were much older now, that was true, and he didn't have much of his own hair left but something about him had given her a suspicion that she was in the presence of the real thing. His slip of the tongue was added evidence. Then when she saw him walk out in front of the audience even before he started to air those incredible vocal chords she knew by the way he graced the stage and took control with such ease that there was no question about it, he was the original singer.

'See you in the pub then, Fay,' Eric called over, hastily putting on his jacket.

'Possibly, I've got some finishing off here to do first,' she replied.

'You work too hard, you know that'.

And with that the young electrician was off through the swinging wooden doors and out of the stage door.

The door to dressing room No 1 was once again set slightly ajar as Fay approached it for the second time that evening. She knocked politely, but no one answered. Slowly she opened the door and saw Ian, who had already changed into his jeans and T shirt, sitting alone at the dressing table, staring ahead at his reflected image. The face that stared back at him was the one he had tried to ignore over the passing years because of a vain reluctance to learn to live with the inevitable. But there was no hiding here in front of the crown of dazzling light bulbs that surrounded the edges of the dressing room mirror. The pain of closely observing his fading features now etched with the signs of exhaustion from the toll of the earlier, high-energy performance was self-evident.

'Was everything alright for you and the band?' Fay asked.

But he still didn't answer.

'Ian, are you all right?' she added, instinctively calling him by his name.

The former superstar's eyes looked upwards to see Fay's reflection join him in the glass.

'So, you knew it was me,' he said, realizing the game was up.

'Well, there only ever will be one of *you*, however good a likeness vocally no one could even come close. But you don't need me to tell you that surely?' Fay replied.

'No, although I'll never be what I once was.'

He stared back again at the stark reflection that to him displayed such cruelness in its accuracy.

'Then you'll just have to learn to accept it, or...' Fay said knowing she was taking a chance with her next sentence, '...wallow around feeling sorry for yourself and go back to what you're now famous for, being a recluse.'

'Got any suggestions for where I go from here?' Ian turned himself around on his chair and saw that he was facing a very capable and pleasantly attractive woman.

'Loads, but the pub on the corner will do for starters,' she told him, making her way towards the door.

'Sounds good to me,' he replied raising himself from his chair. But before following her, he took one last look at the synthetic blonde wig, before swiftly pulling it off of its block and discarding it into the waste bin.

Sweetness Soured

At the age of twelve, I was still a regular tomboy. Having no brothers or sisters, I mainly played with the Ward boys, in the back alleys that stretched behind our Victorian terrace of converted maisonettes. David, the freckled-faced, flame-haired one of the family of five brothers, was my hero and best friend. So, when he told me he was going away that summer to help his uncle who lived and worked on a farm in the country, I felt devastated.

'I'll write to you and I'll even get you a present before I come home,' he told me, noticing how sullen I looked when he broke the news.

'Bring me back an animal,' I ordered him, fighting back my rising emotions, 'nothing else will do.'

And the mischievous imp of a boy that he was did just that.

On the first Sunday in September, the day after his return, he appeared on our doorstop with my coveted gift. I immediately detected something hidden under his jacket, and it was only when he pulled back the turned-down edge of his collar that I saw what it was, a rather scraggy and dishevelled looking duck.

'You know your father will go through the roof when he gets home,' my mother said, watching it quack and waddle round and around in the kitchen. 'He'll tell you it'll have to go, you mark my words.'

'I don't care, it's *my* present and I want to keep her,' I said with defiance, 'and anyway she's special, she's an Aylesbury duck, and they're the best, David Ward told me so.'

'She's not a bad looking bird, a bit on the thin side, but with a bit of feeding she'll soon plump up,' said my father observing her over the edge of his glasses after returning from the pub and his Sunday lunchtime drink.

'Aylesbury duck you say, Marian?'

'Yes,' I answered him, and waited with anticipation for his verdict.

'Well, if it keeps her happy, I don't think it'll do any harm,' my father replied, looking across at my mother who like me was totally surprised at his reaction.

'But bear in mind that you'll be the one who'll have to look after it, not your mother,' he added with a note of caution.

I took up the challenge gratefully, and immediately set to work scrubbing her clean to remove the last traces of the farmyard. She didn't seem to mind and enjoyed the water in our old tin bath, especially the final rinse. But it was a warm towel from the Flatley dryer that really appealed even more. I rubbed her dry with it quickly and firmly to reveal the softness of downy feathers, and then made a makeshift bed from a woollen jumper until I managed to get her some straw. Plonk, being the natural name I thought for a duck, was what I decided to call her, and very soon she and I had forged a companionship that was to become a serious rival to David Ward in the best friend stakes.

A few days later, my mother made an ersatz collar from a leftover piece of leather she had kicking around in a drawer, and plus some old rope, I had the perfect lead for taking my feathery companion for daily walks round the block after school. Quizzical stares and silly remarks in our neighbourhood soon stopped once the novelty of regularly seeing us together wore off. Far from being an oddity, when finally accepted, we were greeted in the same manner as the local dog owners in the area, and that really gave me a sense of pride.

Then one Saturday, late in November I recall, I caught my father feeling her increasing plumpness through the wooden slates of the pen he had made for her out in the scullery. When he realised that I was watching, he got up rather stiffly and walked over to speak to me. I could hardly believe what he had to say, it all sounded so abhorrent. He did attempt to break it to me gently and gave the reasons why he had allowed me to keep the Aylesbury duck from the beginning. But as a naive young girl, I had no notion she was only being allowed as a temporary pet, and that come Christmas she would be destined for the dinner table. An unholy row between my parents took place that morning, and after all the noise and shouting finally settled down, my mother took me aside and tried to explain my father's rational, and I realised that I had to accept the inevitable. But I was far from happy.

Naturally, I didn't look forward to Christmas that year. I tried to imagine that he wouldn't kill her, but I knew I was only deluding myself. On Christmas Eve my father got himself ready for the task ahead, and although capable, when it came to the time his nerves started acting up. After telling my mother to keep me out of the kitchen, he stood outside the door smoking one of his thin cigarettes of loose tobacco, hoping that it would help him to carry out his intentions. Finally, he felt ready and went inside, and within a few seconds I could hear my poor pet calling out, as well as the continuous sound of her flapping wings as she tried to defend herself from my father. Eventually after what seemed like ages, I was unable to take the torment any longer and finally managed to wriggle my way free from my mother's grip and rushed to the kitchen door. But when I opened it, I was unprepared for what awaited me inside. There, running around in front of me but minus her head, was my duck. She'd had it rather badly chopped off by my father, who from the look on his face wished to god he had never decided to do what he had just done.

Then the unenviable task of trussing and preparing what had once been my companion for our apparent festive dinner, fell like her tears to my mother. I had watched her cry before, but never like this. She didn't need to tell me not to remain in the kitchen as I had not the slightest intention of doing so and went away silently to my room to go and cry too.

Christmas Day arrived, and at two o'clock the unwelcome meal was served.

'Eat it Marian', my father ordered me, 'There's not many people who'll be having duck today, think yourself lucky.'

With reluctance I slowly placed a small piece of dark brown meat into my mouth and tried to chew. But feeling like a traitor I spat it right out again onto my plate.

'Here, what do you think you're playing at young lady,' my father shouted at me.

'You're cruel, and I hate you. She was my friend and you killed her!' I screamed at him and got up swiftly, running out of the kitchen and down the stairs, before slamming the front door of the house brusquely behind me.

Years later when I was much older, I realised that, through my father's eye, my duck was only ever regarded as highly prized food destined for the table of a struggling, working-class family. However I never forgave him for what he did to my pet, for it scarred me for life, and nothing he ever did to try and make up for his actions that Christmas was able to change my view.

A Satisfied Customer

I had decided not to go to one of my usual haunts on this particular afternoon for my in-between break after the matinee and before the evening show. Instead, I rushed out of the stage door, crossed over by Piccadilly Circus and disappeared into the back streets behind the Windmill Theatre. I had two hours, well two hours and thirty minutes to be precise if I added in the half-hour call before I was on stage for the evening's performance of the show that I was appearing in. I was playing yet again a 'supporting role' and understudying not only the leading lady, but also covering for two lesser roles in the production. It was a good show, with an excellent and happy cast who, although I mixed with after the performance on occasion going for a drink to one of the many late-night bars, I rarely ate with any of them on matinee days. Sometimes, usually a Thursday matinee, I would meet up with a friend from another show and we would have a meal together, more often than not in Chinatown. But today being Saturday, I was on my own and had decided to try and find somewhere different to eat. Spoilt for choice is one thing that those of us working in the West End certainly were when it came to getting a meal. I walked through the tourist-filled streets passing tacky shops pressed tightly together with the exception of one or two of quality and one that had tailored suits on tailor's dummies in its windows, all made to measure or bespoke as it was officially known in the trade. Then I caught sight of a place that I hadn't really noticed before and crossed over to get a look at the menu pinned up in the window. This wasn't a restaurant as such, it was really a cafe, and had the name 'Solly's' above its door and written up across one window were the words 'Salt Beef'. Through the glass it looked inviting, so I went in.

It was very small, with the counter for takeaways at the front and less than half a dozen tables or so for eating in towards the side. I sat down at an empty, red Formica table, squeezing myself into a chair that was pushed up against the back wall, and picked up the menu. I had on occasion eaten Jewish food for as a child my mother had worked at one time as a waitress in an establishment along the lines of this one, near our home close to Stamford Hill in North London, hot, salt-beef sandwiches being the order of the day. I didn't really need to study the menu; I knew exactly what I would order.

'I'd like a bowl of lokshen soup, and a salt-beef sandwich on rye, plus a glass of lemonade please.'

'Are you Jewish?' asked the old man who came over to take my order, looking bemused.

'Do I have to be to appreciate your food?' I replied.

He shook his head and smiled.

'Forgive me but it was the way you spoke, I don't usually have Gentiles who ask for that particular type of soup,' he told me.

I then told him a little about my mother and the salt-beef bar she had once worked in. His eyes lit up with interest as he listened to my recollections, before he went over to give my order to the cook out the back. He had to be Solly the owner, as he looked so very tired from long hours spent over the years of taking orders similar to mine, or from hundreds of other people all wanting takeaways of bagels filled with smoked salmon and creamed cheese or chopped liver. While I waited for my food, I looked around noticing the clean though worn lino on the floor and the old, faded photographs on the walls. Some looked like they could be family ones from the 50s and others of groups of people all having a good time eating plates of food in the cafe. Tonight, the place looked virtually empty, and apart from myself, I could see only one other person, a greying man in a dark overcoat with a trilby hat by his side, drinking a cup of coffee. My lokshen soup came, hot, filling and truly delicious, and fond childhood memories went flashing through my mind with every spoonful. Then a slight rush of cold air brought me back to my unfamiliar surroundings. I looked up and noticed that the door had opened and a woman had walked in. She was round about thirty-five, beautifully dressed in a tightly fitted, plain navy suit, which showed off her figure to perfection, and in one hand she carried a neat little bag and a pair of gloves. Her fetching face was immaculately made up and her sleek, black, glossy hair was cut short in what used to be called an urchin cut. She looked a picture of elegance and to all intents and purposes a little out of place in the cafe.

My salt-beef sandwich arrived just as she took a seat at the table in front of mine. Her hands pulling down at the sides of her skirt a little as she made herself comfortable. I nodded over to catch Solly's attention and mimed with my hand for a cup of coffee. Before bringing it over, he took the order from the woman and then went back behind the counter to prepare my drink, making up a bagel into the bargain as he did so. I sunk my teeth into the succulent, salt-beef sandwich, a pleasant change to what I usually ate after a matinee.

'Your shoes are very stylish, very stylish indeed.' The man in the overcoat remarked to the woman in the navy suit. 'I have never seen such a quality pair, they look superb,' he told her.

The woman didn't speak or for that matter make any movement with her facial muscles to indicate that she was flattered by such compliments.

'Would you mind if I looked more closely at the workmanship?' he asked.

He got up from where he was sitting and came over to sit at the table next to her. She indicated nothing other than a full stretch of her right leg, to which the man gave a slight gasp, catching his breath as she did so. His gaze was totally transfixed on her foot, or more importantly on her shoe. It was black, rich glossy black leather, like the colour of her hair, with a pointed toe and a heel of five inches or more, rounded off with a tiny metal tip. I watched with interest as the man moved himself nearer to the woman's leg, his eyes not moving their focus from her shoe. Slowly she started to move her foot up and down in a light circular movement as if she were embarking on a set of exercises. Round and round went the foot, first to the right and then to the left. With hawk-like clarity the man's eyes stared on. By now she had him enthralled with each turn of her heel. With outstretched hands he leaned forwards within a few inches of the shoe-clad foot.

'Please, could you permit me to feel the leather?' he said hurriedly.

The excitement in his voice was unmistakable.

Again, the woman made no sound or any form of verbal communication, instead she reached down to her foot and removed the shoe, holding it out to him. I watched intently as he took it from her and cradled it in both hands and in doing so both eyes closed tightly, and his whole body shook with a slight shudder. It was then that I felt that I was a witness to some strange, almost ritualistic vision happening in front of me, as I saw how the man was starting to touch the shoe. His fingers gently caressed the leather, firstly around the body of the shoe itself with sliding, stroking movements in part similar to how one might give affection to a feline. Then his hands explored the soft, light-beige leather lining that filled the inside. Although I had heard that there were people with shoe fetishes, I had never before come across one in the flesh, or to be precise one in action with the object of their desire.

The face of the woman looked blankly across at the spectacle before her, still no expression, nothing, except total control of the situation there but inches away from her. Calmness and command at all times were hers, there was no mistaking that. The man was now fingering the heel and massaging the part where the heel joined down to the long thin point. The index finger on his right hand sliding down, right down to the very tip itself, to the silver metal stud. And then he let out yet another gasp, that sounded like a form of release and in doing so, he drew the shoe quickly to his chest hugging it tightly to himself, and rocked back and forth like a baby, turning his head sideways in towards the collar of his coat as his did so. Stifled sobbing sounds came from his mouth while the gentlest of tears slid down his cheeks, falling into the shoe itself.

'May I have my shoe back please,' said the suited woman, and raised a palm-upturned hand.

The man's eyes fluttered as he gained his composure and in doing so returned from wherever his mind and the object of his desire had transported him.

'Thank you so much, I am most grateful.'

He placed the shoe into her waiting open hand. She reached down, crossed her leg over one thigh and put the shoe back on, easing her foot slowly into it as she did so.

The man raised himself and pushed his chair away.

'It has been a real privilege for me, such an unexpected pleasure.'

And with those final words he turned away from the woman, only pausing to place some coins by his empty coffee cup and to pick up his hat before he went out through the door, disappearing into the crowds outside.

The suited woman's order came, it was a small cup of coffee which she drunk as if to quench a thirst. Then she took out an elegant, enamelled makeup mirror from her bag and checked her appearance. Her hand ruffled through her hair and as I watched I noticed her lips part in a wry smile, at the small reflection gazing back in the glass. In a matter of seconds, it was snapped shut and placed back to where it had come from. Once more she pulled the edges of her skirt down as she stood up to leave, and like the man before her, placed some money down before she too vanished somewhere into the maze of streets outside.

I finished my sandwich and drank the last of my lemonade then realizing the time and that I only had ten minutes to get back for the half-hour call before the start of the evening show, I got up and went over to pay Solly at the counter for my meal.

'Did you see what was happening over there?' I indicated with a nod towards the empty tables.

'Oh yes.'

His reply was somehow matter of fact as he gave me my change.

'What did you make if it?' I said, putting the coins in my purse.

'I would say that he was a satisfied customer,' he replied, with a look in his eyes that conveyed that in one way or another he had seen it all over the years.

And as I hurried out into the damp of the early evening air, I felt that I too had to agree with him.

The Woman of Stencils

It wasn't an imposing house from the road, in fact, it resembled all the others by way of its age and design. Not the type at all that we had originally had in mind, and if it hadn't been for the gentle persuasion of the pleasant young woman at the estate agents, we wouldn't have agreed to go and view it in the first place. She said that she was sure that we would find the house rather appealing and, although she herself couldn't quite put her finger on what it was about this particular property, it certainly had something extra. It also had a good-size kitchen, which was high on our agenda, large rooms that got a propensity of the daylight and a very low-maintenance garden which more than indicated that it was on the small side, so ideal for our requirements. Plus, the price was relatively cheap for a property of its proportions. So then, as my husband was quick to note from the details, if it was such a find why had it been on the market now for almost a year? The location was ideal, close to the sea front in a very desirable road in an attractive coastal town, the sort of place that would normally have been snapped up by any number of house hunters. I myself, drawn by the sound of the place, didn't feel that we should immediately dismiss the property and insisted that at least we gave it the once over, for the fact that it had been lying in wait for so long like a wallflower of a girl waiting patiently for a dance intrigued me and I cajoled my reluctant husband Ian into arranging an appointment.

'Mr & Mrs Roberts? I'm Michael Newton, please, do come in.'

A bright, cheery fellow with an especially thick beard and mop of curly hair, dark brown in colour, but like the hair on his face pepper dusted with grey, ushered us through the door and into a long, salmon-pink-painted hallway.

'Are you alright with cats?' he blurted out before proceeding to let us go any further.

'Oh yes, no problem at all. We've got a couple ourselves,' I replied enthusiastically, as hopefully this would mean that a cat flap was ready and waiting.

'That's good to hear. I always mention it as soon as anyone comes in as, unfortunately, not everyone is a cat lover. Though saying that, knowing our Pipkin he'll be hidden away in the garden somewhere.' Michael Newton turned the brass knob of the nearest door and directed us into the lounge. It was not a particularly light room, so rather disappointing on that score, for naively of me I had expected it to be just as the estate agent had said. Possibly the idly draped, dark red curtains were cutting out the remains of the afternoon sun from the two sides of the bay window, or maybe it was in the other rooms that the brightness excelled. But one thing that I did notice and find extremely appealing was an impressive border that caught my eye high above the top of the paperwork.

'Ah, I can see that you're admiring my wife's stencilling,' Michael Newton said, noticing that my gaze was drawn up towards the ceiling.

'It's a very curious design,' I answered studying the repeated pattern which was really rather splendid.

'Yes, it is, you won't see anything like these. Like all of her work, she designs each one of them herself,' he said proudly.

Michael Newton was not boasting in the least when he spoke of his wife's artwork. For as Ian and I progressed round the house going from room to room, the stencilling started to become even more elaborate and the designs more and more intricate. As we made our way up the staircase, bold leaves with odd-looking symbols embedded in their stems weaved consistently all the way past us like an enormous beanstalk hauntingly convincing in its manner of daring you to follow its path.

'Nearly there!' announced Michael, looking round at Ian and I, and from the sound of his rapid breathing positively relieved to be almost at the end of his tour. This was the third and thankfully final floor, made up of a positively, light-enriching bedroom at the back with far reaching sea views over the rooftops of the houses below, plus a second bathroom and lastly towards the front of the house another bedroom.

'You'll have to excuse my wife, she's busy with a new design,' said Michael gleefully opening the door to the front bedroom to reveal his wife halfway up a ladder stencilling away at the walls for all she was worth.

'Jenny this is Mr & Mrs Roberts, they've come about the house.'

A rather plumpish looking woman just over five feet tall no more, no less, turned around beaming.

'Hello there!' she boomed out and waved across to us from the far corner of the room, before descending from the ladder.

Quick delicate steps, almost gliding like a ballerina, took her rapidly across the shiny, polished, wooden floor to great us. A mauve-paint-stained hand was hurriedly wiped on some rag before giving us both one of the firmest and friendliest of handshakes either of us had received in a long while.

'I'm so sorry that I wasn't able to come and meet you, but I just had to get on with this room.'

'That's Jenny all over,' added Michael, 'once she gets immersed she completely loses track of time.'

'I'm really intrigued by your stencilling, they're such fascinating designs,' I said looking around the walls, before adding, 'the pattern in here especially is very unusual.'

'I'm so glad you appreciate it for it takes a certain eye to really understand the concept,' Jenny Newton replied looking me up and down in the process.

'Well, I think we had better be making a move, thank you very much for showing us your interesting home,' Ian said intervening, which stopped the conversation from going any further. Michael Newton stepped forward to escort us downstairs leaving his wife to happily continue where she had previously left off. We made our way back down along the top corridor with the distinctive beat of her thick, stubby brush tapping the all-consuming stencils still sounding in our ears. Finally just before leaving the house, I snatched a glimpse of a rather overfed, tabby-and-white cat as it ran past our legs, and belted like a shot from a cannon out of the predicted cat flap in the centre of the kitchen door. From my point of view a welcome seal of approval.

'Well, I can see that your enamoured with it,' said my husband as we made our way to our car.

'The estate agent was right, it does have something extra,' I replied, looking back across the street to the house.

'Yes, all that damn stencilling. Don't know what to make about that. A bit overpowering I'd say,' Ian answered opening the car doors.

'Maybe that's the reason no one's bought it. I mean I find it fascinating, but possibly other people wouldn't agree.'

I looked across at Ian hoping that he wouldn't dismiss it for I felt that, now I had seen the inside of the house, I was sure that it was the right one for us. For me it was as if the stencilling really brought the house to life, with every one of Jenny Newton's mesmerising designs more than complementing each of the many rooms. I could imagine Ian and I entertaining in there, with friends remarking and trying to work out what some of the intricacies were on the dining-room walls. I wouldn't want to change things, to do that would feel like a misdemeanour, an insult to all the work that had been so skilfully applied.

'Let's think about it and possibly come back again later in the week. It's hardly going to be snapped up in the meantime,' Ian said, and then, noticing my obvious disappointment, he added, 'Look, Mrs Newton obviously isn't confident of a quick sale or she wouldn't still be doing those endless stencils of hers, now would she?'

We returned the following Tuesday and spent longer in the property this time, asking all the relevant questions. The Newtons told us that they had lived in the house for approximately seven years with their two children Olivia and Josh. Michael didn't mention what he did for a living but Jenny, his wife, said that she was a primary school teacher and the reason for moving was that, although they had all enjoyed living there, it was now time to move on. But whatever their reasons it was not our concern, for by now Ian had realised that there was no question about it; this definitely was the house for us. Fortunately, after our offer had been accepted, Ian agreed with me about the stencilling, that it would be a crime to remove it once we were the new owners.

It was the best of days when we moved in with everything going decidedly better than either of us had expected. Our furniture fitted well into the house and, although there was quite a bit to unpack, the house started to take shape very quickly with our things. In the kitchen we found a very delightful 'New Home' card from the Newtons and written along the bottom a P.S. saying if we saw Pipkin could we let them know and they would come and collect him. He had got out of the rented property they had moved into which was in the same area and they thought he might have returned.

On our third night in the house just before six o'clock when I was putting down some tinned cat food for our own cats, Monty and Fifi, I noticed a face glaring through the cat flap. It was Pipkin who had crossed two roads and walked the length of the street to get back to his former home. I knew of course that cats were capable of such feats, some covering amazing distances to return to where they had previously been living. Though on seeing me he immediately bolted. Feeling concerned for him I felt obliged to put some food down for him outside. I knew that neither of our two cats would be keen on any form of confrontation when they were eventually allowed to venture out into their new garden and, although our male cat Monty had a very distinguished name, he was none the less a complete and utter push-over, and not one to instigate or indeed enter into any cat fights over territory, new or old. Fortunately, I had previously locked the cat flap to keep our two felines inside for the next few weeks so they would get accustomed to their new environment and not stray. So, although Pipkin could look, he certainly couldn't get in even if he wanted to. Back inside the house I telephoned the Newtons and within ten minutes, Michael Newton had arrived armed with some dried cat treats and a cat carrier. Eventually after much effort, the rogue cat was captured, placed inside and the lid firmly shut.

'Well, that's the last we'll see of him,' said a relieved Ian, as Pipkin was put into the back of Michael Newton's car.

But it wasn't by a long chalk. In fact, sightings of him in our garden became quite a regular occurrence. And to make matters worse our own tomcat Monty (once he was allowed out) and Pipkin rather surprisingly become the best of pals. This led to catching the Newtons' cat becoming even more difficult as the pesky creature started resisting not only the cat treats, but also any attempt to be caught and I started wondering just how long this whole charade was going to go on for.

'I'll have a word with the Newton's,' said Ian one Sunday after Pipkin was seen in the garden yet again.

'I thought I'd make the suggestion that maybe he might be better off being re-homed,' he added.

That did seem a sensible idea and one which I agreed would solve the problem.

The house although effectively quiet when empty and devoid of any sound, didn't in the least feel hollow to me when I was left there all alone. On the contrary, it felt very welcoming and alluring, especially the almost mystical stencils spanning the walls. Unconsciously I had started to develop a rapport with them alongside the familiarity that was taking shape with the various rooms in the rest of the house as I effortlessly got used to living there.

'How did it go?' I enquired eagerly, catching sight of Ian coming into the hall from where I was preparing some fruit for a salad in the kitchen.

'Fine,' he said before removing his jacket and placing it in the cloakroom under the stairs along with Monty's pet carrier which he had used to transport Pipkin back to his owners.

'How did they take your suggestion?'

'They seemed to prefer the idea of him staying here,' Ian said, looking somewhat defeated, adding 'Apparently according to Michael Newton he always slept outside in the old shed at the bottom of the garden. He said that he was more of an outdoor cat, really, and tough as old boots. They even said they would contribute to his food which he used to prefer to eat in the shed itself. Funny way to go on if you ask me.'

'You were gone for a while; did they offer you a drink or anything?' I was curious to know more about this family.

'Yes, as a matter of fact Michael Newton did. Had a beer with him in the garden. He seems a solid enough chap. Very pleasant.'

'Did he say what plans they have, for buying another property'?

'No, didn't mention it. Come to think about it, we didn't talk about much in depth, just general things really. Oh, though he did say that they were planning on going back to visit South America. Apparently, the whole family are interested in a recently discovered civilisation. Some sort of tribe, that's similar in part to the Aztecs, but located in a completely different region.'

'Um, I wouldn't mind hearing more about that. Did Jenny Newton come and join you?'

'No, she didn't. In fact, from what I've seen of her I don't think the woman ever has a rest! She was up that ladder of hers stencilling away like mad in the hallway when I got there. Very odd if you ask me, especially as they're only renting.'

I tried to put the Newtons out of my mind, though every time I glanced up at the elaborate borders in each of the rooms in our recently acquired home, my imagination started to get the better of me. I had some very fanciful ideas, some quite ridiculous really, with the impression of Jenny Newton being almost on a mission with her stencils, as if she intended to leave her mark on positively every house that she'd lived in.

Things settled down to an even pace and a slightly new way of living, which is a natural form of adjustment that comes with any change of residence. And for a time, I thought that even Pipkin had decided to accept an alteration and acceptance in his own new accommodation. Until that is one afternoon when I was returning home from doing some late shopping. I had just started walking down Harbour Lane when I saw him. He was heading in the direction of our house, or to him his old residence. So by the time I had got in and put my bags away and opened the back door, there he was sitting like a china bookend by one side of the shed, presumably waiting for it to be opened. I was not in the mood for pandering to his whims. So pretending to go towards the door of the shed to undo the bolt, I swiftly made a grab and scooped him up into my arms, before hastily carrying him indoors and depositing him in Monty's old pet carrier, which as luck would have it was in the utility room at the time after being cleaned out after Monty's check-up at the vets. Much as I quite liked the Newtons' cat, I felt he needed to be back where he belonged, with his rightful owners. After all, surely the Newtons' children must want him back I thought to myself.

'Ah, the wanderer returns! Come on in round the back.'

Jenny Newton's distinctive voice called down to me from out of an open window as I rang the doorbell.

I went through to the garden and was surprised to find the kitchen door open. Although the town was relatively low on crime, it was not something that I myself would have considered doing. I went inside and immediately was struck by what I saw in the kitchen. Stencilling, the like of which was taken even further than in our house, with this time the designs carrying onto the walls themselves. I placed the carrier down carefully in the middle of the room, letting a somewhat disgruntled Pipkin out and waited for Jenny Newton to appear. Again, I heard her call out, this time for me to come upstairs as she had something she wanted me to see. Obediently I made my way out into the hall, before making my way up the stairs of this unfamiliar house. More designs, some extremely vivid, were flowing right down from the border virtually lashing against the paintwork, making me wonder what on earth the driving force was behind this extraordinary style of art form.

'I'm in here!' Jenny called down from upstairs. 'In the front bedroom.'

It didn't come as any surprise to me to see her armed with her beloved stencils in her hand. Only this time she wasn't up a ladder tapping them out onto the walls with her brush, she was actually making the stencils themselves, sitting on the floor drawing them onto paper so that the room was literally covered in cut outs and designs. Some were really exquisitely executed, though others possessed more than a hint of garishness with their peculiar looking patterns. I noted that she was dressed in the identical clothes to when I had first met her, a long-sleeved, black, rather loose-fitting, shapeless dress, with accompanying similar shaded, black stockings on her legs and delicate, little, soft looking, satin-type slippers, the colour of baby pink, on her tiny feet. Its statement was that of the kind of look adopted by a woman who has no intention whatsoever of bowing to the dictates of fashion.

'Well, what do you think?' she said, stretching out her short arms either side of her in declaration.

'I'm almost lost for words,' I replied truthfully, 'As I said when I first saw them, I find them all tremendously fascinating, captivating in fact.'

I astounded myself, not only by my enthusiasm but also by my reply.

Jenny Newton beamed.

'So captivating that you'd dare to have a go?'

She picked up her stencilling brush and held it out coaxingly towards me. The sudden invitation was not what I had expected. It reminded me of a childlike challenge, something that maybe I shouldn't be getting into for fear of where it might lead.

'I'm only a spectator,' I replied, 'you're the expert. But I would like to know where you get your influences from for your ideas for the designs.'

Jenny Newton got to her feet and moved leisurely over towards me. She had the look of someone about to confide in me with a secret.

'They all have their roots with the Tantelouc people who once lived in South America. They used to use them as homage to their various gods, with each one having a distinct variation that spoke only by design and symbol. The actual ones are so utterly compelling, they line the walls of recently uncovered temples and remains of dwellings.'

She pointed at some very interesting stencils laying only inches away in front of my feet. 'See these, now they are something completely different, these are a design based on those that would have been done as a gift made to the god of Cochnaei. Extreme worshippers would be expected to go one step further and succumb to having their entire bodies completely tattooed with them, therefore making the ultimate sacrifice.'

As my eyes followed the run of the pattern, it seemed to draw me in with its beguiling, flower-like swirls and started to make me feel rather heady and as if I was somehow being consumed.

'I really think that I had better make a move,' I said turning my gaze away from the intoxicating pattern and over to Jenny Newton, 'thank you so much for showing me your work and telling me about its origins,' I added politely, before making my way out of the room, feeling the urgent need to get outside for some air.

'It's very rare for me to meet someone who is so moved by my work,' said Jenny Newton as she opened the front door to let me out. I smiled back loosely at her complement.

'Thank you for returning Pipkin. Oh, and do come back again and then I'll show you some more of my designs,' she said reaching over to shake my hand vigorously in farewell. And as she did so, I saw the sleeve on her arm start to ride backwards revealing the skin underneath which was entirely tattooed.

After that day I never once saw or came across any of the Newtons again. Although as fully expected their invincible cat made another return journey, but this time it was decided that he could stay. For like the engrossing stencils on the walls inside the house, he too was to become a permanent fixture.

Luscious Lily

She'd been christened Lillian, but preferred the name Lily, which really did seem to suit her much better. Everyone knew her as Lily, and never Lil, no, no one would ever dream of calling her that. Lily she was and like a lily she became. Tall, svelte with porcelain skin, green eyes and a cascade of rich, chestnut-coloured hair, that was Lily.

She was a cut above the rest of the local girls who lived in the village and, strangely for such a small place, no one tried to pick holes in her or talk about her behind her back, possibly because she was such a lovely specimen of womanhood and a credit to the local community. People far and wide knew of Lily or Luscious Lily as the local men liked to call her. So luscious was she with that full, red mouth of hers appearing to dare someone to place their lips over it and kiss it, and feel its warmth on theirs, so gorgeous was she this walking sight for sore eyes. But Lily had other things on her mind far and above the reach of anything as mundane as kissing.

She was a quiet, young girl who was always helpful to the elderly people living nearby, running errands for them and collecting their prescriptions. How lucky they all were, for none of them knew quite what they would do without Lily. She was always obliging and nothing was too much trouble, except for Mondays, of course, everyone knew she made time for herself on Mondays. But what they didn't know was what she did with that time.

Raymond Dale was a well-known artist who lived in an old converted schoolhouse with his wife Cynthia, though most people knew her more than they did him, the reason being that Cynthia was a very chatty type of woman and Raymond was a man of few words. They were both artists from good backgrounds, having met many years ago when they were both teaching at the Slade. Money was no object, as they had acquired enough from Cynthia's father's estate after his death and decided to move out and make a fresh start in the country.

'Oh, there you are! We were getting anxious and thought you weren't going to come tonight,' Cynthia said opening the front door, extremely relieved to see Lily standing there. Lily gave her a faint smile as she passed her by before going straight upstairs into Raymond and Cynthia's bedroom, where she closed the door and started to take off all her clothes. She emerged a few minutes later in a dressing gown, before going down the stairs and then into the living room.

'Take your time my dear,' said Cynthia, 'and just do whatever feels comfortable, and if at anytime you need to stop, remember, just let us know.'

Lily walked into the middle of the room, and untied her white towelling dressing gown, pausing for a second before she let it slip to the ground, and then she slowly laid herself down amongst the pile of cushions that were strewn around on the floor. 'Exquisite,' thought Raymond to himself, as he picked up his pad and started to draw. His hand frantically working away sketching the fine lines of Lily's body, every curve and muscle and twist of her wondrous female form was put to paper as quickly as he could before she took up another position.

'She's the best model I've ever drawn, her form is perfection,' said Raymond as he tore off the finished sketch from his pad and tossed it down beside him. The other artists in the room all nodded in agreement. As well as Raymond and Cynthia, the others were George, a nervous man who painted mainly as a hobby and two women, Daphne and Julia, whose works were seen on occasion at local exhibitions in the area from time to time. Only Raymond's work was anything of note, more than a cut above the rest, and as well as being acclaimed for his drawings and paintings, it was his sculpture work that really was of the essence.

'Shall we have some short poses, Raymond?' asked Cynthia.

‘I’d rather we had a long, reclining back pose, if everyone else is agreeable,’ he replied, and then added ‘any objections?’

Nobody in the room disagreed.

‘Lily,’ said Raymond, gazing straight at the girl, ‘Is that ok with you?’

Lily didn’t reply, she seductively turned her body around and over so that she was lying on her stomach, her head turned gently to the side with her arms under her, and her long legs stretched out the full length of the cushions. Her ability to hold a pose for sometimes up to forty minutes was remarkable and gave each artist the greatest of opportunities for defining their drawings. Unfortunately for Raymond, the evening as always was over far too quickly for his liking. The two hours that Lily modelled seemed not long enough, and Raymond’s frustration at this was more than apparent that night. He could hardly wait for her to appear again after she had gone upstairs to dress, for he had something that he desperately wanted to say.

‘Here’s your money, Lily,’ he said rushing over to her when she came back downstairs. He handed her two notes, one for twenty pounds and the other for ten. The girl took it and put it straight into a small, red leather purse.

‘I can’t believe how quickly tonight has gone, I was wondering if you could spare a few extra hours, say of an afternoon?’

Lily raised her eyes and held Raymond’s gaze. ‘To pose for me that is. I have something rather special that I’m working on,’ he then added, ‘of you that is, and I really need more modelling time to complete it. Of course, I’d make it worth your while moneywise as it would be a private session.’

He smiled a wide, opened-mouthed smile in anticipation that the extra remuneration would get her to agree.

‘I’m only free on Mondays,’ said Lily, and with an almost sarcastic tone added, ‘as everyone round here seems to know. But I could come here again some Wednesdays if, as you say, you’d make it worth my while.’

Raymond could hardly contain himself with his excitement, which was apparent in his voice.

‘Oh, that’s splendid, really splendid,’ he said joyfully. ‘Say from two till four and I’ll give you £40 for your time.’

‘£60,’ said Lily quite adamantly.

Raymond saw the determination in Lily’s face and was not prepared to argue in case she turned him down.

‘Sixty pounds it is then.’

This time it was she, Lily, who smiled.

‘Well, I’ll be off, see you Wednesday, Raymond.’

And on that note she was gone.

And so Lily made an exception to her otherwise routine way of life in the village and started to visit the schoolhouse most Wednesday afternoons as well as Monday evenings. The arrangement suited Raymond well, as Cynthia was out of the house doing her various charity work, and he had solitude to work. But most of all was the accomplishment of having Lily model for him exclusively. He produced sketch after sketch of her, then progressed to using oils in thick bold strokes in complimenting colours, working harder than he had ever done in years, and at the end of each completed work he felt an inner sense of achievement and satisfaction. He was now drawing Lily in his private studio, adjacent to the main part of the house, where no one came, not even Cynthia. Also, for the first time in years Raymond had started a sculpture, a life-size one of Lily lying in a reclining pose with just a slight twist to her body.

‘Perfect, perfect, just hold that,’ said Raymond in an almost hushed tone.

His hands worked effortlessly, striving on and on trying to match his sculpture to the real-life form of the beautiful, young woman’s body. This body intoxicated him like nothing he had ever experienced before, her translucent skin, her contours, and the fullness of her breasts. Then there was her hair, that wonderful chestnut hair, and those eyes of hers which conveyed such an air of seduction, which Raymond was now remarkably transferring to the clay model.

'You enjoy modelling don't you, Lily?' said Raymond one Wednesday towards the end of the afternoon.

'I find it relaxing if that's what you mean,' Lily replied, without moving.

'Oh, I think it's more than that,' he answered. 'I don't believe it's just for the money, it's for the power isn't it?' 'I'm right am I not?'

At this point Lily turned, got up, reached out for her dressing gown and started to put it on.

'You're very observant, aren't you, Raymond?' And with a toss of her glorious, sweeping mane of hair she went out of the room to dress.

And so they continued, artist and model, working together in close harmony, both artists in their own right, he with his skillful hands, and her with her lithesome body, like a dancer, an artist of the stage, with both of them complimenting one another in the production of art that excelled everywhere around Raymond's studio. There was no intimacy of a sexual nature in their relationship, no far from it, it was higher than that, it was a meeting of like souls who were tuned into the same wavelength. Both of them getting pleasure from the liaison, she of power to captivate him with her features, he enthralled with the beauty of it all, trying desperately to bring this captivation to his art.

By the beginning of the autumn the sculpture was finished, and Raymond made secret preparations to have it shown at the Annual Art Exhibition for the region, which would take place as always at the Old Guildhall in the adjacent town. It was the first time in years that he had entered, let alone shown a life-size figure. No one knew about the figure, not even Cynthia, who assumed his entry was going to be of one of his paintings. She herself felt her own work was not up to any previous standard, and therefore not good enough to be exhibited this year. Amongst their friends, Julia had entered a watercolour of the local stretch of river, Daphne, a painting of a village churchyard done in oils, and George had been persuaded to submit a painting of his sister's hands resting on the keys of a piano, which was rather well executed and pleased him no end to think that he had been encouraged to enter it.

The day of the exhibition finally came round, with everyone taking their works to the main hall and then setting about the task of displaying them. Everyone's except Raymond's, because his work had already been taken to the hall the previous night. It had been carefully transported there with Raymond supervising the entire operation and the placing of the sculpture centre stage in the middle of the hall. The opening was packed with artists and the usual types one always saw at these gatherings. Art as we all know has been defined many times as being a matter of taste, and something that many people cannot agree on, but there was no mistaking the agreement in the hall on the sculpture of Lily. The crowd of people that flocked to stand around the nude sculpture was staggering, with expressions that showed amazement, not at the subject matter itself, but for the way in which it had been shaped. That was what made them linger admiringly at the skillful definition of beauty, so that it amassed more onlookers than any other exhibit in the hall.

'It really and truly is sensational,' said Cynthia as she approached her husband's side. 'I am so proud,' she told him, adding, 'of you both.'

She smiled lovingly at Raymond who was standing just a short distance from the crowd.

'Your delight in her is evident in your work. Only now are you truly artistically fulfilled.'

Raymond turned to his wife and took her hand, 'I knew that you'd totally understand.'

Credit where credit was due. Without Lily there would not have been such an alluring model, and without Raymond there would not have been the hands to work the clay and deliver such a work of excellence. After the exhibition was over, he gave the sculpture to the town and it was installed in the entrance to the Old Guildhall for the world to see. Everyone in Lily's village was extremely proud of it, and proud too of Lily, who waited till the initial excitement had died away before she ventured into town to see it for herself. Approaching the entrance of the Old Guildhall from the main sweep of steps she walked in, in typically Lily fashion, almost gliding up the steps and along the polished, black-and-white, harlequin-patterned, marble floor which was at the front of the building. And then she saw it, her image, no it was more than that, it was her, frozen in time, looking out from the sculpture with a seductive gaze that only Raymond could have captured. Ever so slowly Lily approached her remarkable resemblance and as she did so, the people surrounding it moved aside to make way for her. They knew instantly who she was for there was no mistaking her, as she was so distinctive. She scanned every inch of the likeness of herself, as if she was in some way scrutinizing it for any imperfection. None was to be found. Lily smiled to herself, and then she saw the inscription that had been written in the clay by Raymond, as the finishing touch to his work:

'Luscious Lily' - The Power of Perfection,
by Raymond Dale.

Lily tossed her hair back over her shoulders and, as she turned to go, smiling with as always her assured air of self-confidence, there was now added something more, something she'd never had before. At last in her possession was the feeling of total satisfaction.

The Fame Game

It wasn't the first time that she had seen his face outside a West End theatre. The last time he had been wearing a wig, of that she was sure. But now his hair was visibly grey verging on white, and the very short cut accentuated how little there was left of what she had once remembered.

Brian Stanway, the name sounded as solid as it was written in thick, bold letters under his photograph which was mounted behind a glass cabinet. In the corner of the wood surround was carved a tiny lock, hardly visible unless a person was astute or they were like Wendy, who had also once had her photograph in a similar frame and would have known of its precise whereabouts. She stood briefly studying this familiar face, of someone whom she had once regarded as a good friend. Now he was a real somebody in the acting profession, with scores of successes in London as well as two highly acclaimed performances on Broadway. Oh, how different it had been nearly thirty years ago, she thought to herself, when the boot had been firmly on the other foot. Then it had been her turn, her name up there and he, well he at the time was only just beginning.

They had met in the same production in which she was the female lead, and he had the very least to do, claiming that the director didn't think much of him as an actor. But Wendy did and, determined to help him, introduced Brian to influential friends and contacts, essential for a young man on the look out for a step up. Their friendship lasted only as long as was necessary, to him that is, and once Wendy started to find that the parts just weren't there any more as younger actresses were taking her place, the opposite was happening for Brian. Suddenly he was on a roll, with casting directors all clamouring to get him for any number of productions.

It wasn't that they had ever been a couple, their togetherness being purely and simply platonic. So, when the end came as it did almost without warning it was she, Wendy, who suffered as if from losing a close relative. The signs had been there for a while, of course; his excuses for not returning her calls had become so transparent that she didn't know why he even bothered. Then, when by chance she found out that Brian had sold his flat and moved without even letting her know, the realisation that their friendship was finally over hit home.

Walking away from his smiling image and quickening her step past the stage door and on down St Martin's Lane, Wendy consoled herself with the knowledge that she was not the first and probably not the last person that this would happen to. Her only regret was that she could never go and see him performing, because the unforgettable past prevented this from ever happening.

Remember, Remember

Although it wasn't the best of areas that this city had to offer, it certainly wasn't the worse. And because I hadn't yet learned to drive in those days, the early 70s, the options open to me for transport were either finding out which was the right bus to take or ordering myself a taxi. I waited impatiently outside the telephone booth at the stage door for the use of the only phone in the building available to us artists, assorted crew and various members of the touring production that I was in at the time. I looked again at the name and address that had been hastily scribbled along with the phone number. The shaky hand of George, the stage door keeper, had written it down for me only a few minutes before. I usually had my accommodation sorted out in advance but not this time, relying instead on a recommendation from the resident stage door keeper.

After a short wait, I went into the booth and made my call. The voice on the other end was that of a long-standing theatre landlady, a dying breed so to speak even then.

'Is that Mrs Hutchinson?' I enquired. 'Yes, it is, who's calling', the voice that answered sounded kind with a gentle, Brummie accent. 'I'm an actress working at the theatre and I'm in need of accommodation for the run of our show'. There was again a slight pause and then she replied. 'Would it be from tonight?'. 'Yes', I said. Again, a slight pause. 'I'm a bit of a way out but on a bus route stopping at the top of the road, if you're sure that wouldn't be a problem'. I thought I detected something in her voice, I wasn't sure but wondered if she was in some way trying to put me off from staying there. 'Oh no, that's not a problem, and there really isn't anywhere else, I think all the other digs have been taken,' I told her, not that I knew if this was true or not it was just my assumption based on the fact our show was made up of a large cast, plus musicians and crew and I imagined most of the digs especially those nearer the theatre would have been taken. 'Well, in that case if you can come now, I'm in all afternoon.' She told me what bus and where to pick it up in the city centre and to just ask the driver to put me off at Elmsfield Road.

It was true it certainly was a bit of a way out, a good 25 minutes at least before we got to my destination. It was a long road but fortunately number fourteen was near the top.

It was from the front what I would describe as a pleasant-looking house, Victorian-terraced, strong-looking walls, reasonably maintained outside and clean net curtains in the windows. Good first impressions. There was a large pot of skimmia placed near the door and in the front garden a small patch of lawn with assorted plants, nothing fancy or bright, all neatly placed around its edges. Very orderly, as was the rest of the house when I went inside. It was old fashioned which was no surprise as many of the landladies of a certain age I had stayed with during this long tour had homes similar. It was as if time had stood still in all the rooms here, stood still from another time in the life of Mrs Hutchinson.

My landlady to be was a rather thin woman with short, tidily-set, permed, grey hair, around about sixty-five, or maybe older or even a bit younger than I had put her, it was so difficult to be accurate as mature ladies in those days tended to look older than their years. She was neatly dressed in a lilac blouse and mauve cardigan and was also wearing what used to be referred to as a sensible skirt, not something I would ever dream of wearing as firstly I was not one for skirts, preferring tight denim jeans or long, flowing, flowery dresses in my early twenties, and two - I was not someone who as a young woman could ever be thought of or referred to as being particularly sensible. Mrs Hutchinson wore an apron and, like all the other landladies I ever encountered during my career when staying away in theatrical digs, it appeared to be part of her identity, like a uniform that she would put on each morning.

'I'll show you the room,' she said after I had come in and we had exchanged a few words, or should I say I did for Mrs Hutchinson, although not unfriendly, seemed not a great talker and rather on the quiet side.

The room was a reasonable size for a single, with a neatly-made-up bed in one corner. I noticed it had freshly starched, white cotton sheets and pillowcases and a burgundy-coloured eiderdown on top of blankets, and next to it a small bedside cabinet. A wardrobe and chest of drawers were by one wall, also there was a worn but comfortable-looking wingback easy chair and a small table and hardback chair by the window. I walked over to it and looked out. Below was a medium-sized garden as neat and as tidy as the small front one. An old fireplace with a Victorian surround caught my eye, it was in the centre wall in the room, it had a two-bar electric fire in front of it and on its shelf on either side were a couple of Hornsea ornaments, Flora Royal, one with a squirrel and the other a deer, both animals nestling by rose-and-leaf-entwined tree trunks. Above the fireplace on the wall hung a rather stark painting of the Cob in Lyme Regis as it was on a rainswept day, but it was, I thought, quite well done. Experience had given me an eye for noting what was acceptable and what was not in theatre digs and this room, although rather old fashioned, was clearly acceptable.

'I'll take it.' I said to Mrs Hutchinson adding 'It's a nice room and I'll be able to write my letters home looking out over your pretty garden.'

My new landlady gave the start of a slight smile, obviously pleased at my wanting the room and my complement. 'There is one other person living here, a permanent lodger, Mr Maynard,' she informed me. 'I doubt you'll ever see him. He works in the city centre in the day, goes home Friday to see his wife as he lives too far away for daily commuting and back on Monday evening.'

I was then shown the bathroom and the dining room downstairs where I was to have my breakfast which I arranged for 10am each morning, unless I wanted it earlier or even much later which would be no trouble I was told and to just let her know or leave a note by the side of the clock on the sideboard. As a theatre landlady Mrs Hutchinson would have a complete understanding of the needs of a performer.

The weekly cost for bed and breakfast was very reasonable. I did think it was rather cheap and, in fact, the cheapest digs I had found so far on this tour which I had already been on for over seven months with another five to go. I paid for a week in advance (I would be staying for three in total) and was handed a door key. Mrs Hutchinson offered me a cup of tea but I said I really had to get back to the theatre for our dress rehearsal and needed to get my dressing room sorted out plus collect my suitcase which was on one of the theatre trucks. I asked her if I could ring for a taxi and she gave me a number to call. The taxi was going to take only about five minutes to arrive, so I said I'd wait outside and then told Mrs Hutchinson I'd be back later on that evening. She seemed to start to warm and told me that when I returned I could make myself some toast or help myself to biscuits and tea or a hot cocoa and could do this every evening on my return. I thanked her and then left the house and stood by the streetlamp to wait for the taxi. While there I noticed three young children around about ten, two boys and a girl, with an old cart and a rather battered guy in it which they were dragging along the road near to the house. It was the first of November, only a few days away from Guy Fawkes Night. I heard one of them call out to a man passing them, 'Penny for the guy, Mister!' but they had no luck. They then went and knocked next door at number twelve, again there was no answer, and then they bypassed Mrs Hutchinson's house and went to the other side number sixteen. This time they were in luck as someone answered and they were given some money. My taxi arrived and after I had got into it and it had pulled away I thought it a bit odd that the children didn't knock at Mrs Hutchinson's door but then imagined maybe they had done so in the past and she wouldn't give them anything, it did seem a reasonable explanation but in actual fact it was far from the truth.

My dressing room in this particular theatre was fortunately close to the stage and it didn't take me long to get my bits and pieces sorted out and my stage makeup, brushes and other essentials arranged on my dressing table. I always loved seeing the light bulbs on all around the dressing room mirrors and, for once, not one of them needed replacing. They spoke of the theatre to me, of being an actress in show business, someone who had arrived and, although not a well-known performer, I had an enviable role in this production that many other young actresses would have coveted. I was playing the leading lady so had my own room which meant more space and also somewhere I could make very personal during the three-week run in this city. The dress rehearsal went very well, only a few stops and starts and then I was free to go. I'd eaten a really good lunch at midday in a cafe near the theatre and now after the dress rehearsal I had a sandwich and cup of tea in the wardrobe room. Joan, our lovely surrogate mum of a wardrobe mistress, had made a variety of sandwiches for anyone in the cast who wanted them and we certainly did. It was good to sit down and chat with her and also to other members of the cast who came in and out. After a while I went and retrieved my suitcase from the dock area of the stage where they had all been put after being unloaded from one of the theatre trucks. I then hauled it to the stage door and rung for a taxi to take me back to my digs.

By taxi it took no time at all to get back and forth to Elmsfield Road and this one taking me back really drove swiftly along. I thought of Mrs Hutchinson imagining she never went in a taxi, only ever using the bus which would be the reason she had told me it was quite a way out. Although it was now getting quite dark, children were still out in the street knocking on doors, a different gang this time who were across the road from me and also with a guy in tow in a cart hoping they too, like the ones I'd seen earlier, would get some money even if only a few pennies to enable them to buy some fireworks. After I had got out of the taxi and it had pulled away, I heard the children singing as they walked along pulling their cart behind them, 'Remember, Remember the Fifth of November.' It sounded like a chant, over and over again they sang the words and then they started to giggle to one another with their hands cupped over their mouths. I opened my bag to look for my new door key; fortunately, the lamp outside in the street helped me as the light it gave off enabled me to locate the key easily. As I came into the house, I could hear a radio playing some classical music in a room downstairs, it was not loud and rather quite soothing. I made my way up to my room dragging my suitcase up each stair and then once inside I unpacked. As I started to hang my clothes in the wardrobe, I realised that it was rather on the small side and more suitable for a child. It was possible to hang my clothes in there but a couple of long dresses draped down so I had to use two extra coat hangers to take up the bottoms. Just as I was hanging up my spare jeans, I noticed a glass marble right in the very corner of the back of the wardrobe. I reached over and picked it up and brought it out into the light of the room. In the palm of my hand I felt the coldness of the glass. I had played marbles as a young schoolgirl and now remembered that period of time in my formative years as I gazed at the glass ball in my hand. It seemed a rather odd find and rather puzzling as to what it was doing in the wardrobe. I decided to put it back where I had found it as it seemed to me something that had been there for a long time and destined to stay there for even longer.

After I had put out the rest of my personal belongings I read for a while and then made my way downstairs to make myself a cup of cocoa. I noticed there was a light on in the room opposite mine as I passed it in the hallway, Mr Maynard's I presumed, but there no sound coming from inside. The room at the front, the main bedroom, would no doubt be that of my landlady.

I went to bed that night earlier than I would usually do at around 10.30pm, for normally at that time except for the day of a dress rehearsal I would have only just come off the stage from the show. But I felt very tired from a morning travelling up from London, checking out my digs for the run, then the dress rehearsal, it had all taken it out of me. The bed I found to be quite comfortable and the sheets so cool to the touch of my skin that I was soon asleep. I must have slept for quite a few hours and then I awoke from a disturbed dream centring on a group of disconcerting children playing with marbles in a playground that left me in a bit of a sweat. I sat up and looked around the room, there was some welcoming light coming in from the window as the curtains were not lined. This did not bother me, in fact I found it rather comforting. My eyes wandered over to the wardrobe and I started to think about the marble that I had earlier found in there. Where did it come from and whose was it? Unanswered questions that I could not answer. I laid down and cleared my mind and eventually fell asleep again, this time into a deep sleep.

I awoke the following morning before the alarm clock went off which was unusual for me. I lay there in my new surroundings for a while wondering how many other theatricals had stayed in this room over the years and what had become of them. I glanced over at my clock and moved the switch to off. I got up and went over to the window and pulled the curtains back slightly, just enough to see what sort of day it was. It was dull, a grey sky, rather dismal but not to be unexpected for early November. I headed off to the bathroom and then got myself dressed quite quickly, the room not being very warm I didn't want to linger, unlike back at home with my parents in North London where I would have stayed in my dressing gown most of the morning.

Mrs Hutchinson had obviously heard me when I had got up for as I entered the dining room there was already a pot of tea waiting for me. A neatly embroidered, clean tablecloth was on the table and everything set out for breakfast including orange juice and a selection of cereals all just for me. Mr Maynard I presumed having had his breakfast quite a while before me, although there was no sign, no indication that anyone else had eaten there.

'Did you sleep well,' Mrs Hutchison asked bringing in my toast.

'Yes,' I replied, 'Though I did have a strange dream, I expect it's because it's new surroundings, I replied.

'What was in your dream,' she asked.

'Oh, something about a playground and children playing with marbles. I expect it was because I saw some in the street doing penny for the guy.'

Mrs Hutchinson's face took on a serious demeanour.

'Anyway, it was only a dream,' I told her, 'Just a mix of things from the day.'

Mrs Hutchinson didn't reply, so I thought it best to change the subject completely.

'I imagine you have had many theatricals staying here,' I asked her.

'Oh yes, over the years,' she answered rather abruptly. I didn't get the impression she wanted to expand on this and decided not to ask any more questions. She then went out of the room only returning with my fried breakfast. After I had finished, I complemented her on what I'd just eaten and she gave me a brief modest smile, but her eyes didn't light up and I felt overall she looked quite forlorn.

The show opened well that evening and, as was normally the case, we took the city by storm with our performance. We'd become used to standing ovations over the many months of the tour and we received them from the first night onwards. It really felt good to be in such a hit so that being away from home and living out of a suitcase was bearable as the reward for performing was immense. Back at my digs, the next three nights I slept better than the first though I wouldn't say I had the best of sleeps, but at least I wasn't experiencing any more strange dreams. On the Friday night, as I came back in a taxi, I saw and heard the last fireworks going off every so often all along the route back to Elmsfield Road. It was, of course, the fifth of November, bonfire night or Guy Fawkes as some people called it. I imagined the children whom I'd seen knocking on doors for pennies for the guy previously in the week had had their fireworks much earlier and were by now all tucked up in bed. As usual I made myself a cup of cocoa and took it up to my room before going to bed. It had been a long week and tomorrow after the two shows on Saturday I would be going straight back home for the weekend getting a lift from another cast member who, luckily for me, also lived in North London. So tonight, I looked forward to getting a good night's sleep and, after getting into bed, I quickly fell asleep. But I could not have been asleep for very long when I was woken up by the sound of a child screaming. For a moment I thought I'd been dreaming but sitting up in the bed with my eyes open I could still hear it. The sound was extremely disturbing as if the child were in pain, serious pain. I felt a chill run down my spine as what I was hearing sounded as if it was coming from downstairs. I put the bedside lamp on and looked at my alarm clock, it was just after 1.00am. I got up quietly and put my dressing gown on and went out into the hallway and slowly made my way to the top of the stairs and listened. But as I did so the screaming suddenly stopped and the downstairs was eerily silent. I retraced my steps and went back to my bedroom and sat in the wingback chair. My heart was now racing and I was trembling all over. I started to rationalise what I had heard. It must have been either a bad dream or the sound from a child living next door. I tried to convince myself it was one or the other but couldn't. I knew exactly what I had heard and it had come from this house.

Eventually I went back to bed and at some point managed to get to sleep but not before questions had gone round and round in my head and I knew the only answer to them could be found with Mrs Hutchinson.

The next day was extremely bright and sunny for the time of year, the sort of day to make everything seem cheery, a day to take pleasure in. But I didn't feel lifted by it as I got up, nor as I made my way downstairs to the dining room for breakfast. I had rehearsed in my mind what I was going to say to Mrs Hutchinson, although the moment I went into the room I was unsure of how to broach the subject of what I had heard in the night. I didn't feel particularly hungry and said I would just have some cereal and toast. Mrs Hutchinson looked concerned and asked me if I thought I was going down with something, to which I said no. Finally, I could not contain myself any longer.

'I was woken up last night by a child screaming,' I told her firmly, adding, 'it sounded as if it was coming from down here.' This was not the way I had wanted to say it but this was how it came out.

Mrs Hutchinson caught hold of the table, in fact I thought she was going to faint and then she composed herself and sat down in the chair facing me.

'What you heard was my son David,' she said and as I looked over at her I could see her face had turned quite pale.

'But it was the sound of a child not an adult,' I said with puzzlement. 'Look maybe I was wrong and it was from next door.'

'You were not wrong and there are no children living next door. No children on either side. It was my son's voice you heard when he was ten years old.' Mrs Hutchinson spoke the words with conviction.

I then realized what she was saying.

'So, I heard a ghost?'

She nodded and looked over at me with such sadness in her eyes.

Like last night I suddenly felt another chill run down my spine as I realised the house had a haunting. I didn't know what next to say so waited for Mrs Hutchinson to speak and eventually she did. She then started to tell me the story of what had happened to David, so many years ago in 1950 when he was just a child of ten. It was the most terrible tale I had ever heard.

She told me how David had been playing out with some of his friends late in the afternoon on Bonfire Night. They then went further down the road to where a bomb site had previously been, now built over with flats. A large bonfire had been built there earlier by some adults and perched on the top was a guy and later on it was where a bonfire party with fireworks was due to take place. All the children were looking forward to it, especially David. Some of them had been going out collecting money for fireworks doing Penny for the Guy, but David was not one of them as her late husband Arthur had refused to let him go saying it was a form of begging. The children were an assortment of ages but there was one boy of about fifteen who had joined them who no one seemed to know. This older boy started to light bangers and throw them around so the children were shrieking and laughing and running to avoid them, and then he lit a firework and held it in his hand for a while and then threw this too. He then singled David out and lit another firework and offered it to him to hold, but he refused knowing the danger. Suddenly the older boy shoved the firework into one of David's pockets, but before he could remove it the firework exploded. David collapsed to the ground screaming and with his clothes on fire.

Mrs Hutchinson stopped speaking for a couple of minutes to wipe tears from her eyes before continuing with her painful story.

She then told me how some neighbours who were walking nearby rushed over and threw a coat over him to put out the flames. They then carried him back home and brought him into the dining room placing him gently on the table.

I looked over at the table in front of me imaging the horrific scene that must have taken place all those years ago in this room and I shuddered.

'I cut his trousers off, but the firework had caused such terrible damage to his little body,' Mrs Hutchinson told me, 'And he just kept screaming and screaming,' she added, obviously reliving everything all over again. 'There was nothing I could do, nothing. He died on that table,' she pointed directly at it, 'with his head cradled in my arms.'

I wished there were something I could say that would take away her pain but there wasn't. I also knew that when I spoke I would need to tread softly with my words.

'I take it the police found the boy who was responsible?' I asked my question as gently as I could needing to find the ending to this sad tale.

Mrs Hutchinson shook her head from side to side. 'No, he was never found, he just disappeared.'

I thought for a moment before I responded.

'Does the screaming only happen every year on bonfire night?'

'Yes, and if anyone who's staying hears it, I always say it's a child next door, which they always accept. But I could tell you really knew it wasn't, that is why I told you the truth,' Mrs Hutchinson said with frank openness.

'Mr Maynard, has it woken him?' I enquired.

'Mr Maynard is never here on the fifth of November, it's his wife's birthday so he always goes home for a few days.'

'And do you ever hear it?' I asked her.

'Always,' she replied looking directly at me.

That night and every night afterwards I had surprisingly good sleeps and never again woke in the night or was woken up by any sounds whatsoever. Then one morning as I was leaving the house, I came across a next-door neighbour at number sixteen, an elderly man whom I'd never seen before. He was tending to his front garden and after I had said hello we struck up a conversation. He was very interested in the theatre and told me how, over the years, he had seen many theatre people come and go from Mrs Hutchinson's and said how exciting a life it must be. I told him that it was and then asked him if he had any children to which he said no, he was a widower adding his late wife had wanted them but he said they had not been lucky. I then asked about the house on the other side number twelve, if any children lived there to which he said the lady was a spinster who'd lived in the house all her life firstly with her parents and now as a pensioner. He then gave me a rather peculiar look as if he was wondering as to why I had asked these questions or possibly because he knew of what went on in the house I was lodging in on the fifth of November. I had no way of knowing and I didn't want nor need to ask anything more so I wished him a good day and went on my way.

I never spoke again of what I heard that night to Mrs Hutchinson and neither did she to me. I also decided not to tell anyone involved with the show. I had my reasons, not just because I thought they would not believe me but because I had been made a confidant and with that comes a trust I was not prepared to break. It is only now nearly fifty years later that I have thought it an acceptable time to tell this disturbing story. Mrs Hutchinson will no longer be alive and neither will either of her next door neighbours. The house will now have new occupants, possibly more than one family will have lived there during this last half century and I expect there will have been many children in the house too and maybe there still are. But every time when the fifth of November comes around, I remember what happened that night at fourteen Elmsfield Road and wonder if the haunting still continues or if it has possibly passed. I have no way of knowing. All I do know is that what I heard and what was told to me by Mrs Hutchinson has never left me and it never will. So now I carry it with me, not as a burden but as a remembrance to her son and to his lasting memory.

The Egyptian Head

Julia had already left the charity shop when she decided that she was going to turn around and go right back in again and this time buy it. If of no real value, then it was hardly going to cost her anything, except for five pounds fifty. Being a bit of a gambler, it wasn't much of an outlay and, of course, the shop would at least benefit.

'This is very unusual,' said the elderly female assistant who took the head from her. 'Looks very old too.'

'Um, yes. Any chance of getting a bit off the price?' Julia asked adding, 'There's some damage above one of the eyebrows.'

She pointed it out to the woman.

'Fifty pence is all I can take off. I shouldn't do that really,' replied the assistant nervously.

Julia handed a crisp, five-pound note over, and waited impatiently for the woman to wrap up her purchase and give it back to her.

'I don't think it's worth anything', said her husband Robin when he looked at it. 'It's certainly not marble and definitely not Egyptian.'

'How do you know?' Julia replied somewhat affronted.

'Well, I'd be very surprised if it was, or if there was any value attached to it,' he replied scathingly before placing it down on the coffee table.

He was right that it wasn't an original Egyptian Head from the time of the pharaohs as Julia had hoped but, nevertheless, it was not without worth. For after she had taken it to Willoughby's, the local auction house, they had called in an expert and two weeks later the history that was attached to her find was revealed. It had been sculpted in the 1920s by Picasso and was the only piece of its kind that he had ever produced. It was said that he had given it to one of his muses and that after her death no one knew where it had ended up, until now.

Julia wasted no time in having the head auctioned at a top London auction house and was ecstatic when she heard it go under the hammer for three point five million pounds. Shortly afterwards both her and Robin's lifestyle changed accordingly as would be expected of people who suddenly come into such a vast sum. But the money instead of making them happy beyond their wildest dreams as they had expected, brought with it a whole range of insurmountable problems. Endless arguments rapidly took place even before the cheque was handed over and deposited in the bank about where to live and what sort of house they were going to buy. Julia insisted on a swimming pool whereas Robin, who couldn't swim, didn't see the point in having one. Like two over-indulged teenagers, the bickering continued even after they bought a desirable house and started living their new life.

Less than four months later they decided to get divorced, as it seemed the only solution and the only thing that they could both agree on without arguing.

Boy Dancer

It was many years ago that all this happened, when I was appearing in one of London's long-running musicals, the name of which is not important to this story, suffice to say that it had been a huge hit with the public when it first opened. But to most people in the business (show business that is) it had been on for far too long and was now looking somewhat tired and jaded like some faded, former grand hotel, still trying desperately to hold on to its dignity by living off its past glories, while not accepting the inevitable with grace and admittance that the best had long since gone and that, sadly, its time was nearly up.

I had come into the production to play a supporting role and had signed a contract for a year's guaranteed run, being brought in with three others to replace some performers who had just left and, it was hoped by the management, inject some new life into the show itself. I was put into a dressing room with seven other women singers down a long, dark corridor badly in need of more than a lick of paint. It was near the top of the building on the third floor with a large sash window that looked out over the heart of Soho. On the front of our dressing room door there was a small, typed card that said simply 'Girl Singers' and just along the corridor from us another room with another card, this one saying 'Boy Dancers.' This room housed some of the most extrovert, theatrically talented and experienced male dancers in the entire West End at that particular time, all cramped together in two ridiculously small rooms knocked into one, with two hand basins at one end and masses of full-frontal pictures of naked young men adorning every conceivable spare inch of wall at the other.

The ages of these dancers ranged from early twenties to mid-thirties and beyond to someone known to all as the 'oldest boy dancer in the business', the wickedly outrageous

Rex Morris. Naturally I had heard of Rex, amongst us artistes he was a legend in his own life-time, and although I was known for being able to hold my own under any given situation, I was more than a little apprehensive about coming face-to-face with him for the first time. Part of his reputation was that he was known to possess a tongue as sharp as the cutting edge of a barber's razor and, apparently, if someone crossed him, they would soon know all about it. On the other hand, he was known to be loyal and generous to those he liked and who liked him, fun to be around and above all else to be a superb dancer. I can remember vividly when I first met him or when, should I say, he introduced himself to me. I was doing the rounds of the dressing rooms, as you do when you are the new recruit, being introduced to the rest of the cast by the lovely Welsh soprano, Joy Williams, who had volunteered to be my unofficial guide, and who would give me a few tips along the way as we passed through the labyrinth of corridors that made up part of the backstage of the theatre.

'Prepare yourself,' said Joy, as we returned to our own corridor, 'It's time to meet the boys!'

'You mean we're back to where we started. That's a relief, only the boy dancers left,' I replied.

'Yes, I thought I'd save the best for last,' she answered, and added, 'Don't look so worried, they may bite, but they won't eat you!'

She giggled as she knocked twice on the dressing room door.

'Come!' boomed out a loud voice, more of an order than a welcoming greeting. Joy turned the handle of the door and in a split second we were inside. The smell of heavily perfumed air was the first thing to hit my nostrils; it was an array of only the very top men's fragrances, the best that money could buy. In the room the boy dancers were all in various stages of undress, some were sitting around reading or smoking, some going about the business of getting prepared for the evening's performance, putting on their slap (theatre term for make-up) and some were busy preening themselves in front of the various mirrors.

'Hi everyone, meet our newest addition to the show,' said Joy light-heartedly.

'My, my, aren't we lucky!' said a voice somewhat sarcastically, observing my reflection in one of the dressing room mirrors. The dancer was making up his hair with some white powder to make it look grey, although his eyes continued to watch me as he looked into the glass.

'So, you're one of the gang of four brought in to get a few more bums on seats,' he added while starting to work on his sideburns.

'That's Francis,' said a nice-looking, young, blond-haired man, 'just ignore him. I'm Alain Stevens by the way,' he added, stretching out a hand in greeting. 'Love your perfume, darling, Chanel isn't it?'

I looked at his friendly-looking face.

'Yes, as a matter of fact it is. It's No 5.'

'Ooh, tell me, do you wear it to bed *a la Marilyn*?' Alain's eyes lit up as he said this.

'I'm afraid I'm not with you,' I answered unsure as to what he was getting at.

'Marilyn Monroe,' replied Alain. 'Apparently, she slept naked as a blue jay, except for a dab of her favourite perfume,' he told me excitedly.

'I don't know why *you're* getting your pants in a lather, you old queen, *you'd* run a mile if you ever came close to a naked woman, whether she was wearing No 5, or had scrubbed herself down with a bar of carbolic!' The put down and delivery was first rate and could only be from one person.

'Hello, Mr. Morris, I've heard so much about you,' I said, turning to face him.

'And you're *so* pleased to meet me,' he quickly replied finishing my sentence for me as he started to look me up and down.

We stood there surveying one another like two animals from the same species meeting for the first time, both weighing each other up. I remember noticing that he was shorter than I had imagined, although he carried himself extremely well with a straight back and erect head, which gave the illusion of added inches, so vital to a dancer. His features were as sharp as his reputation was - high cheekbones, strong nose and bright, sparkling brown eyes. His dark hair was cut short, closely cropped to his scalp and quite severe so that it accentuated his face, which sported a well-cared-for bushy moustache.

'So, you're one of the season's latest additions,' he said gazing straight at me. 'Tell me, are the rumours we're hearing about you true?'

Everyone else in the dressing room seemed to have stopped what they were doing to listen. If I now gave the wrong reply, I knew that my time in the show would be a tough one.

'What, that I've got more front than Brighton?' I spoke the sentence fast, and confident in my Cockney accent.

Immediately a shrill laughter went up around the dressing room. I felt on to a winner and looked round at each of the guys in turn.

'You ain't seen nothing yet, boys, just wait till the house lights go down!' I told them.

The dancers continued laughing as each one of them eagerly rushed up and surrounded me in a circle, all of them showering me with warmth and good luck wishes for my first night's performance.

Rex waited till they had all calmed down and then approached me again. Once more he stood in front of me, but this time he reached out and took hold of my chin with his right hand and turned my face from side to side as he did so.

'Nice cheekbones, bona face and a rumour I've heard is you've got one of the best voices around, too good for this poxy production. I like your style and, believe me, there's more than a lack of that around here at the moment,' he said, his eyes darting around the dressing room.

'You doing anything after the show?' Rex enquired. Though again he didn't wait for me to answer.

'Well, if you are, you're going to have to cancel it, because you're coming out with me and the boys tonight, we're all going down to one of my favourite haunts, where we'll really let our hair down.'

'Thank you, Mr. Morris.'

'Oh, listen to her, cut the formality, it's Rex,' he told me. Then added, 'Knock 'em dead tonight darling, give the bastards their money's worth. We'll all be gunning for you.'

And then he hugged me and gave me a theatrical kiss on my cheek, which more than indicated that I was going to be one of the gang.

I certainly did as Rex suggested and knocked 'em dead that night. My role, although a small supporting one, was reasonable, and I also had the advantage over the rest of the other female singers in that I had some nice solo lines to sing in one particular number with the leading man. At the time I had been around the West End musical scene for nearly twelve years, and although I'd been fortunate in one or two productions to play decent leading roles this show wasn't one of them, and due to finances and the fact that I had been out of work for more than six months, I had agreed to go into this long runner which as well as the small part included the inevitable chorus work. I knew only too well that for me it was a bit of a come down and, like quite a few of the cast, felt frustrated with my lot. It seemed to me that the profession was like a game of snakes and ladders and after nearly getting to the top with a couple of ladders left to climb, I had encountered more than my fair share of snakes and was almost back to where I'd started. Such is life.

'That's another one done!' said Francis as we started the climb back up to our respective dressing rooms after the final curtain call.

'How long you been in the show, Francis?' I asked.

'Too long,' he answered, giving me a weary look as he started to unbutton his stiff collar. And then he said, 'For what it's worth, it'll be five years come next month. I'm not complaining, just stating a fact.' He gave me a half-hearted grin and continued to undo his shirt as we kept on climbing the stairs. Then Alain suddenly appeared alongside me having taken the stairs two at a time.

'Hi, honey, you were fabulous, and your voice was terrific. Shame you haven't got a solo, now that *would* be something.'

He rushed past me, ripping off his vest.

'I'm going to race Francis to the shower tonight, see you at the stage door.'

When I got to my dressing room the girl singers were very sweet and opened a bottle of champagne to celebrate and toast me as their 'new recruit.' Joy poured it out into glasses and we drunk it down quickly as we started the job of removing wigs, costumes and finally make-up.

'So, you've been honoured with an invitation from Rex tonight,' said Joy as we both started to wash ourselves down in the basins at the back of our dressing room. There was only one shower on our floor, to be used by both men and women alike; tonight I was quite content to forego waiting to use it, especially as I didn't know how long Francis and Alain might take.

'You'll be there too, won't you?' I asked Joy.

'I'm not the one whose been invited, anyway I really couldn't make it tonight as I'm getting a lift from Marcus, one of the male singers, but I know you'll have a smashing time, and besides you can tell me all about it tomorrow evening.'

'I get the feeling that there's more than a possibility I'm going to be the only female,' I said as I wiped myself down with my towel.

'You could be right there, in the true sense of the word that is!' replied Joy chuckling as she said it.

Suddenly a boyish head popped round the dressing room door.

'Joy, are you coming, I don't want to be stuck in traffic down the Old Kent Road.'

'Two minutes, Marcus, and I'll be right down.'

Joy hurriedly pulled on her trousers and top and within an instant she was ready to go. 'Bye all,' she called out and then she looked over at me, 'Have a great time,' she said smiling, and quick as a flash she was gone.

Downstairs, the stage door had an assortment of people waiting around it that night. As well as a few die-hard fans and long-suffering partners, there was a handful of cast members from other shows and, of course, the boy dancers who I would be joining alongside Rex. They were all there decked out in their clubbing attire, with tightly-fitting, black leather trousers seeming to be the order of the day, fitted shirts and black leather waistcoats and jackets, topped off with immaculately washed and styled hair. I felt a bit like the poor relation standing there in my red velvet dress, but I didn't mind as I knew that I was not part of the competition.

'Nice to see you've put your glad rags on,' said a distinctive voice floating down the stairs. It was, of course, Rex audible before he was even visible.

'Well, I didn't want to let the side down,' I replied as he appeared in the hallway of the stage door. His outfit more than matched the others, for if there was ever chic in a man, he was it, and if what he was wearing tonight was his Monday outfit, God only knows what he saved for the weekend.

'Ready then?' Rex asked looking over at the little group of us. He then turned to me,

'You may take my arm,' he told me as he made a crook. 'Let's go,' he said as I slipped my arm through, and he led me out of the stage door, with the others following closely behind.

Although I had been to a few clubs and bars in my time, I had not been to anything like the one that I was going to tonight. We walked through the winding streets of Soho, which was alive and kicking, with the usual girls hanging out on the corners, and punters and seedy looking men passing in and out of grubby doorways. Lights blazed out of the few remaining strip clubs that were left in the area, an area that I knew just as well by day as by night, as I often walked through it many times during my years auditioning and working in musicals. Bar Espana was still open, the Italian restaurants too, and faint sounds of the last of the audiences rushing off to get their Tube trains home could just be made out in the distance.

'Here we are!' said Rex, as we came up to the entrance of a basement in a building in one of the back streets. 'Follow me if you want a good time, and if you don't then don't bother coming in.'

We all followed.

The doorman seemed to know all the boy dancers and started to let them all pass through. On seeing me however he paused.

'It's alright, Lee, she's in the show, and she's my guest tonight,' Rex said with an authoritarian air.

'That's alright, Mr. Morris, hope you all have an enjoyable evening,' replied the doorman, waving me on into the club.

We all went in with no money being exchanged, presumably being 'in the show' was enough, or perhaps there was a deal going on with complimentary theatre tickets, I didn't ask, I just accepted it.

Once inside, I could see what consisted of an intimate lounge area, including some small, cosy-looking alcoves, and a long bar area on the right-hand side. It was darkly lit in a reddish hue and, as my eyes got used to this unfamiliar lighting, I noticed that the clientele was predominantly male, and that it included a number of transvestites in drag. This didn't bother me in the least, or the fact that I was possibly the only woman wearing a dress there that night. Towards the back of the room I could see a small stage with a piano in its centre and a pianist playing and softly singing the Cole Porter number 'Night and Day.' It all looked rather inviting, especially as it was my first taste of a late-night piano bar. We, that is Alain, Francis, Rex and myself, all sat down by the piano player and ordered our drinks from a passing waiter, the other dancers having decided to go over to the bar area, where they could get a good view of the scene. The pianist played on, playing the number extremely well, possibly because he had played it a hundred times before, or possibly because he enjoyed playing it and was a good pianist.

'It'll be your turn later on,' said Rex looking at me, 'Michael likes to have singers who can sing go up and do a number, it'll give his voice a rest and it will give this lot something to shout about and that will be good for your reputation.'

'I'm all for that,' I answered eager to sing a solo.

In just over half an hour I was up on the small stage belting out 'Love for Sale' for all it was worth. When I had finished the number, the response was so good that I had to do another. I was and had been used to getting up and singing ad-lib for as long as I could remember, from being a small child, and knew countless songs and styles so there was no problem, I just told Michael the song and key it was in and we were away. I then decided to give them the Piaf number 'No Regrets', and gave it all I had, which really brought the place down with its big finish.

'What did I tell you?' said Rex smiling when I eventually returned to where I'd been sitting, 'It's not the Palladium, honey, but you've got yourself a roomful of fans.' He went on, 'And here is one of them,' he gestured towards a tall, young, thin guy with short, sandy blond hair, and a close-cropped beard. 'This is my friend', Lenny.'

After a brief greeting the conversation went through the usual routine of congratulations and then the question of why I wasn't a star with the other dancers all agreeing on how unfair the business could be. All the things I had heard said about me many times before and, without being a cynic, I knew that, unless fate took a hand, like a well-played record I would be hearing this conversation for a very long time to come.

Although he was pleasant and very generous in his praise regarding my singing, for some reason I didn't particularly care for Lenny. There was something about him that made me feel somewhat uneasy, and which gave me an unpleasant feeling in my stomach. He wasn't what you might call to mind as being the immediate choice as a partner for Rex, but then Rex was different to most of the gay men that I knew and from a later conversation with Michael I found out that, although they didn't live together, Rex and Lenny had been a couple for quite a few years.

The night wore on, Michael continued to play the piano and Francis got up and did a number called 'I Hate Men' and then Serena (one of the transvestites) did 'Mad About The Boy', which was a scream all round as she/he camped it up no end, and afterwards Michael sung once again and then played some instrumentals. Eventually the piano bar started to thin out as the couples that had formed slipped away together. I had by now started to get weary as it had been a long night what with my first night's performance in the show and performing down here at the piano bar. Most of the others had already gone a while ago though Rex and Lenny were still there, this time deep in conversation. I got up to leave and Michael, who had joined our table after finishing his set for the night, said he'd escort me to my car.

We said our good nights to those who were left and walked out into the bright light of early morning. There had been a slight downpour of rain and all the pavements glistened with millions of droplets of water. For once the air in the streets smelt fresh and clean like mountain rain and, although I felt tired, I didn't mind the short walk through these streets to my little orange mini as I knew that this was one of the best times to walk through Soho, in the early morning after a light shower.

Michael and I made our way through the quiet back streets towards where I had left my car near to the theatre.

'You certainly made an impression tonight,' he said.

'Thanks. Do you know, I enjoyed myself more singing after the show than performing in it.'

'That's doesn't surprise me,' he answered, 'at least you'll be able to work off some of your frustrations by singing down the Pink Room and be appreciated at the same time.'

'Do you know, that's the first time tonight I've heard anyone say what the place was called, I didn't even know it had a name.'

'Well, that's its official name but it's been called a lot of other things in the past, as I'm sure you can imagine,' he replied giving me a knowing look.

Yes, I certainly could. It seemed the sort of place that had been there for a very long time in various guises and most probably had had its fair share of critics who would have liked to close the place down, even though they had never and probably would never dare go inside.

'Do you need a lift?' I asked him when we arrived at my mini.

'I only live over in Covent Garden, but a lift would be nice.'

I opened the car doors and we got in and then I drove off in the direction of Cambridge Circus.

Michael, a well preserved guy who told me (in confidence), that he was in his late forties, was a pleasant companion at this early hour, and we chatted freely about men and how we had both had our fair share of problems; I having recently got over a relationship that had been a disaster from the start, and he having problems with his present lover who wanted more of a commitment from him. I always found it easy and relaxing to talk to gay men about relationships, it gave me a different perspective and an insight into what makes a man, any type of man, tick.

'Just here will do fine,' he told me as we pulled up outside a row of shops near Endell Street. But before I left and drove home to North London, there was something on my mind that I felt compelled to ask him.

'Michael, I know it's none of my business, but have you any idea what on earth Rex sees in Lenny? There's something about him that makes me feel uneasy somehow.'

'Join the club, honey,' he said dryly.

'Well, thank God I'm not the only one who feels that way,' I told him, feeling glad that it wasn't just me who didn't care for Lenny.

'No one knows much about him, he just appeared down the club one night with Rex about,' Michael stopped to think for a second, 'three, no four, about four years ago. We all tolerate him, but I agree with you. What on earth Rex sees in him I don't know, I mean he's no oil painting, but obviously whatever he has he has it well hidden from view,' he said raising one eyebrow.

I smiled and, on that note, we said goodnight with me promising to come down to the Pink Room later on that week.

It was at the weekend when I went down the club again and, from then on, I started to be a regular and within a few months felt almost like part of the furniture. The passing months in the show seemed to go very quickly and after six months I was rather pleased in that I had completed half of my contract in the show and thankful to Rex for introducing me to the Pink Room which, as Michael had rightly said on that first night, was where I would be able to work off my frustrations. It certainly made the bitter pill of eight shows a week virtually stuck in the chorus more bearable. With Michael's help, I started to work on new numbers as well as old standards and became something of a feature let alone an asset to the place. I got to know the customers and the owner of the club Gordon, a canny Scot, who was keen to have me do a full act down there when my theatre contract was up. It felt nice to be wanted.

With regards to my love life, I had decided to put that on hold for the first time in a long while and, although the life I was leading seemed to go hand-in-hand with erratic affairs, I had decided that for just this once I wanted to be counted out of the latter.

Although now I was a familiar part of the scene down the club, I didn't mix as much as I had initially done with the boy dancers. Possibly because I was making my own crowd with friends from other shows joining in the fun and entertainment, or possibly because the boys were doing their own thing with their own kind, or chatting up any new talent that happened to make its way down to the basement club. Alain still came down, though now he was accompanied by his new friend Karl, the fitness instructor from the gym at the YMCA, and Francis popped in from time to time usually sitting up at the bar looking as he always did like he'd had one too many of just about everything. Rex came in very infrequently, sometimes with Lenny sometimes without.

The show, as usual, went on packing them in.

'When it eventually comes off, I'll have notched up a nice little tidy sum in redundancy money,' said Francis in the quick change room one evening as a few of us were discussing just exactly how long the show might continue running.

'Don't bank on it,' Marcus replied, 'this thing will run for eternity.'

'That's OK by me,' Joy told him, 'At least it's paying my mortgage.'

'And it's just paid for my new curtains and tiebacks,' butted in Alain as he dashed in to do his fourth quick change of the evening.

'What about our songbird?' Francis said looking over in my direction, 'Are you planning on staying till the death, or are you cashing your chips in at the end of your first year's contract?'

I smiled. 'I'll keep you posted,' I replied and then added, 'When I do go though, I hope you buggers will give me as good a party as the Pink Room's planning for Rex on Friday.'

'Oh my God, I'd nearly forgotten,' said Marcus drawing in breath, 'Of course, it's the old queen's fiftieth isn't it.'

'Don't knock it, honey, it'll come to us all one day,' Francis said sarcastically.

'I hope it'll be a good turn out,' I told them, 'Apparently, Michael says that a lot of Rex's old friends will be coming so it sounds like it could be a night to remember.'

If I'd only been able to look into the future, I would have eaten my words.

I remember how the stage door on that particular Friday evening resembled a first night. It was literally showered with cards and flowers for Rex. Huge bouquets and baskets arrived one after the other from old colleagues from all the major musical shows, each of them varying in size and content in their arrangement. Some even sported fruits intertwined with flowers, others champagne, caviar, gentlemen's cologne, the originality and inventiveness in the baskets seemed endless.

Rex certainly wanted to make the most of his birthday and had kicked it off to a fine start earlier in the day with lunch at his favourite restaurant, Geraldo's, which served superb Italian cuisine of the first order. Then he had spent the rest of the day shopping for yet more clothes to add to his extensive wardrobe, before swanning into the theatre to make the most of all the fuss that was being lavished on him. That night's performance seemed to fizz along like the champagne that was being drunk by Rex and whosoever popped into the boy dancers' dressing room during breaks from the performance. I didn't go in for a glass myself, having decided that it would be better to wait and have a drink with him when I gave him my gift after all the fuss had died down and hopefully that moment would be down the club. I had bought what I was sure was the ideal present which was a little pair of gold dancer's shoes made into a brooch. It looked classy and very chic, just like the person it was intended for.

'Hurry up you lot if you're coming!' shouted out Marcus leaving his dressing room, 'We want to get there before the crush.'

'Before the food runs out more like,' Francis called out after him, 'Talk about eat, he never stops, do you Marcus? He must have a bloody tapeworm if you ask me!'

'Shut it Francis or I will!' Marcus replied sounding really annoyed.

'Yes, you and whose army?' replied Francis as he came out to face him in the corridor.

'Pack it in you two,' Alain's voice came in quickly like a referee, 'You go on, Marcus, we'll see you down there.'

'Boys, wait for us won't you,' called out Joy down the corridor.

'I'm ready now,' I said to her picking up my bag, 'We can walk over together'.

Within minutes we had both left the theatre with that evening's performance well behind us and were looking forward to a great night ahead.

The Pink Room was already brimming with people when we arrived, with only a small selection from the regulars of the club, the rest being by invitation only to Rex's private birthday party. In keeping with the feel and name of the place, Gordon had decked it out completely in pink. There was frothy, pink tulle everywhere, with over-the-top, pink satin bows draped around pillars and the front of the bar, and even a special cocktail had been concocted called 'Rex's Revenge', a lethal alcoholic mix with the overall colour an overwhelming shade of shocking pink. There was also plenty of food and wine for the gannets amongst us and the music provided by Michael, who was as usual playing away at the piano. I more than expected to do a couple of numbers, and also had heard that Alain and a few of the other boy dancers had a little floor show planned for later on in the evening. I expected us all to be in for a very long night, partying on till the early hours if all went to plan.

Joy, Marcus and myself found seats near to the piano and stage, then went to help ourselves to some food. When I got over there, I noticed quite a few people whom I hadn't come across before and Joy told me that she thought they might be dancers from the same generation as Rex.

'That's right,' said the voice of a tall, extremely thin and attractively sophisticated-looking woman with a short crop of baby-blonde hair, 'We were dancers, but we're more than a bit past it now. My name's Stella by the way. Years ago, I was fortunate enough to partner Rex in quite a few shows. I teach now and have my own school over in Hendon.'

She took a sip from a glass of wine and cradled it in front of her, her two hands showing off an immaculately painted set of nails, the colour of succulent summer strawberries.

'He's a one-off,' she said smiling, 'but I expect you know that already. An exception to the rule as far as us dancers are concerned is Rex. Whereas most of us had to hang up our shoes years ago, he has the remarkable ability to be able to go on and on.'

Joy and I introduced ourselves to Stella, having left Marcus to the delights of the seafood salad, and very quickly found a rapport with this very pleasant and stylish woman. As Stella was no longer in the business, it was a welcome change not to talk the usual 'shop' centring around the gossip of the current shows that were coming and going and instead hear her talk about her past and the productions that she herself had once been in. She told us how she had first met Rex when they were both appearing in an out-of-town tour of yet another one of those dreadful cowboy musicals, as she called them, the ones that always felt dated, especially when you were appearing in them for nine months or more travelling around the sticks.

'And to keep everyone going, Rex would hold great afternoon tea parties one afternoon a week. We used to have such a laugh, you really had to be there to appreciate them,' Stella told us and looked sadly into the distance as she reminisced.

'Of course, that was in the days of Dennis,' she added.

Stella then went on to tell us all about Dennis. How he had been a theatrical costumier with an Aladdin's Cave of a workshop and premises not that far from the Pink Room where he designed outfits for all the major productions. His forte was for intricate creations with sequins and feathers for the girl dancers, show stopping numbers every one.

Apparently, Rex and Dennis met during fittings for one such show and hit it off instantly.

'They were about the same age,' Stella recalled, 'both very flamboyant, especially in their dress sense, though Dennis was the more serious one of the two. They were inseparable, and it seemed as if they knew exactly what the other one was thinking. It was quite uncanny at times and when it ended it was so terrible for Rex.'

'Did Dennis leave him?' Joy enquired.

'Dennis died,' Stella answered, 'It was a hit-and-run accident. He was crossing the road not that far from here when it happened.'

'Poor Rex. I've often wondered if there had once been anyone really special,' I said. Then I added, 'Before that waste of space Lenny whom he cultivates.'

Just as I finished my sentence a loud applause started beyond the bar area. I looked over towards where it was coming from and saw that Rex himself had just walked in. He looked very relaxed and fantastic in his latest outfit. Lenny was tagging close behind like a bloodhound with his face looking downwards towards the floor.

'Well, I'm going to go and join the crowd. Coming?' said Joy, smoothing out the creases in her skirt and going over to join the tight clutch of people huddled around Rex. Stella and I followed.

Rex was really on top form that night with his one-liners and sharp witticisms. I was very impressed. The crowd around him all lapped it up and then, after a little while, the night's entertainment started. Michael did a medley of Gershwin numbers and I sang 'Nobody Does It Like Me' followed by 'No Regrets' which I knew was one of Rex's favourites. Then the floor show began. Alain and two of his friends decked out in wild, sequinned dresses, voluminous wigs and long, oyster-white gloves appeared on the tiny stage to wolf whistles and rapturous applause from the audience. They did an act that they had devised to the song 'Kiss Me Honey, Honey, Kiss Me,' and halfway through they left the stage and came down and mingled amongst us. Alain then went over to his friend, Karl, the fitness instructor. He teased him with his gloved hands caressing and ruffling his hair, while the other two found more than a willing number of volunteers to be flirtatious with.

The evening continued on the high that it had started out on, with dancing taking over from the floor show. I danced a few numbers with Marcus and then said that I felt I needed some fresh air, and went down the passage where the toilets were located, towards the back of the club, where I knew there was a door leading to the outside, easier to get to than going through the front as it was so packed inside. As I started to walk along the passage, I heard a commotion coming from inside the men's toilets. I could hardly make out the voices from all the screaming and shouting, until the door flew open and I found myself a silent witness, observing Rex as he forcefully pushed Lenny out of the toilet.

'You bastard, you cheap little whore!' Rex spat the words out in Lenny's face, shoving him up against the passage wall.

'After all I've done for you', Rex went on, 'And *this* is how you pay me!'

Lenny stood there motionless with one of the blankest looks I have ever seen on a person's face. He didn't make any movement as Rex continued to push him even harder and then he slapped his face. Lenny just stood there in the dingy surroundings and took all that was being dished out to him.

A young guy in tight-fitting jeans came out of the toilet and slinked past me in the passage grinning when he saw what was going on.

Rex continued to hit Lenny but by then I couldn't hold back any longer and grabbed hold of Rex's arm.

'Stop it, Rex, whatever he's done, don't you think he's had enough?' I said tightening my grip and trying hard to pull him away.

'He certainly has had more than enough from me, that's for sure,' Rex answered letting his arm fall down to his side. His eyes looked closely at Lenny, who was still against the passage wall, with noticeable red weals across one side of his face where Rex's hand had just been.

'If I ever see you again, I will walk right past,' he said almost in a hushed whisper, 'You mean nothing to me, do you understand?'

Rex turned to me, 'Would you be so kind as to escort me home?' he asked me.

I took his arm and as we walked down the corridor, through the door and into the club, Rex flashed me a look which, even if I hadn't been able to interpret it, I would have automatically done what he was expecting of me, that is to keep what had just happened to myself. Somehow we managed to say our goodbyes, with Rex being the good trooper that he was, never for once even hinting to anyone what had taken place. We left the club and found my mini which was fortunately only a short walk away that evening. But just after putting my seat belt on and starting the engine, I suddenly gasped, for there was Lenny's face pressing itself up against the window near to the passenger seat where Rex was sitting.

'Drive!' he shouted, almost like a command.

'I can't, I think he's got hold of the door!'

'Well, he'll just have to let it go won't he,' said Rex sounding unconcerned as he looked straight ahead out of the windscreen.

As I pulled away, Lenny still had a hold of the door and started to run along with the car, and then miraculously he let go and, as I looked out of my rear-view mirror, I could see him standing in the road behind us and within seconds saw that he was hardly visible.

'Where to?' I asked, feeling like I'd just been involved in a bank raid, rather than attending a birthday party, as I put my foot down on the accelerator.

'West Hampstead,' replied Rex.

My knowledge of the areas of North London was pretty good as I came from that neck of the woods, and it was only towards the end of our journey that I needed more specific directions. The entire time I was driving was conducted in silence, I didn't feel that it was my place to pry, that would have been an intrusion, so I just drove. Eventually Rex started to speak, giving me directions and shortly we pulled up outside an old block of flats dating I imagined from the early part of the 20th century. The walls were of the dusty, russet-red brickwork that was distinctive of the period and, as I looked up, I could see that most of the windows had pretty little boxes in them with assorted flowers which took away some of the dullness of the building itself. And then in the stillness of night in that suburban street, Rex started to open up and tell me all about Lenny. It was a story that, even before it unfolded, I wished that I wasn't going to hear. I didn't think it was going to be pleasant and in actual fact it wasn't, it was obscene.

'He was a rent boy,' said Rex, blurting the words out, 'I watched him for weeks, before I approached him. I wanted him, oh, how I wanted him. Not just for a one-off, but for myself, for me, only for me.'

As he continued, I could hear little sobs now starting.

'I loved him, can you understand that, an old queen like me? Don't try to ask me what it was about him, I don't know, I just felt drawn to him.'

I knew before he even looked at me that his guard was finally down. I felt embarrassed, not at what I was hearing, but for the fact that the Rex Morris I knew, or thought I knew, was not sitting beside me, it was a broken man with a shattered heart, a stranger whom I was only now really starting to get to know. He stared at me through eyes full of tears.

'I'm not going to make any judgment,' I told him. 'You really don't have to put yourself through any more torture telling me all this.'

'It's more painful trying to hold it in,' he replied.

'For a while I'd have him all to myself,' he said continuing with his story, 'and then it would start all over again with the one-night stands, and the quick pickups, like tonight. Even on my birthday he couldn't stop himself.'

'So that's what it was in the toilet,' I said.

Rex turned his head and looked at me. 'That's right, a quick blow job with a guy who'd eyed him up over at the bar. Sickening isn't it, even by my standards.'

I then remembered the young guy in jeans who brushed past me in the corridor with a grin on his face during the attack Rex administered on Lenny.

'Would you like a hot drink, I'm feeling rather cold,' Rex asked me.

'Yes, I'd really appreciate a cup of coffee,' I told him.

We made our way towards the vast, ornate double doors that sealed the entrance to the flats within, their wooden panels encased with faded brass swirls of elaborate designs that hinted at a previous illustrious time, long since vanished, of opulence and wealthy living. Once inside we went up some stairs, with my hands touching cold, coal-black banisters of shiny metal with similar swirling designs to the ones on the front entrance. Rex paused on the second landing that we came to that had a series of doors stretching off from it, and I watched him take his key out of his leather jacket and put it into the lock of the most immediate one to us. Once inside I felt an overwhelming sense of suffocation at the interior, which was stuffed full of miscellaneous items and objets d'art. It was as if I had entered a huge antique shop, one of those that houses items of moderate value along with some rather expensive pieces including furniture and china. I hoped that what I felt wasn't sensed by Rex, especially in the light of what had happened this evening, as I didn't want him to be upset any more than he already was. He led me into a sitting room and, as my eyes looked around the unfamiliar surroundings, I mentally started to date various items in the room which seemed to be from the 1900s to just before the Second World War. Then as I was about to sit down a voice called out.

'Moshe, is that you?'

'Yes, it's alright, Mama, you can go back to bed.'

A little, old Jewish woman wearing a long, navy-blue, woollen dressing gown appeared at the sitting room door.

She had come to welcome her son home and as she did so, she reached out to kiss him on both cheeks.

‘Did you have a nice birthday,’ she asked.

‘Yes, Mama, it was very nice,’ Rex replied.

‘And he had lots of lovely presents and beautiful bouquets of flowers, they are all at the theatre’, I replied sensing she would like to hear this.

‘Good, good,’ she said smiling warmly, and then turned her attention on me.

‘My name is Esther,’ she said as she held out her hand. I took hold of it gently as, just like her, it seemed very frail. I then told her my name.

‘Hasn’t my son offered you anything to eat or drink?’ she looked over towards Rex. Although it had to be at least 2 o’clock in the morning, I could tell that hospitality, whatever the time of day of night, was always readily given by Esther.

‘He was just going to make some coffee, weren’t you, Moshe?’ I looked over at Rex with a twinkle in my eye.

‘Coffee, oy vey, it’s more than coffee you’ll be wanting,’ she raised her eyes to the ceiling as she said this, ‘Wait, sit down, and make yourself comfortable,’ she said and indicated to the sofa, ‘I’ll be back shortly.’ And with that she left us alone.

‘Moshe Berkovitch. You can see why I changed it. Alright if I’d wanted to be an accountant,’ said Rex.

I looked towards the door.

‘She’s very proud of you, you know, I can tell. To her you’ll always be her Moshe, the name you were first given.’

He nodded and reached up to wipe away a tear that was already forming in his eye.

Within minutes it seemed that Rex’s mother had returned, with steaming, freshly-made coffee and an assortment of sandwiches and delicious apple strudel.

‘And now I will go back to bed. I don’t want to intrude, I only wanted to hear how the party went. Moshe was so looking forward to it,’ she said and then indicated to the food, ‘Please, help yourself.’

After she had left Rex and I talked, and as we did so, the room and its surroundings started not to feel so oppressive and I almost felt comfortable in this strange and unfamiliar environment.

Oddly, we didn't resume talking about Lenny, it appeared it had been dealt with. Instead Rex told me a little about his years with Dennis, and then after the terrible shock of Dennis's sudden and untimely death that he threw himself into his work and managed to find comfort by continuing with his dancing career.

'My mother accepts I'll never marry. She knows I'm not interested in women and doesn't say much, she just listens, like you've done tonight'.

'Does she know?' I asked.

'What, that I'm gay? Oh yes, she might be an old lady but she's quite liberated, like a lot of us Jews she's led a difficult life.'

We talked for a while longer, with Rex telling me about his family; his deceased father having been a tailor with his own shop, and his mother working there in the back helping with the making of the suits and doing any necessary alterations that might be required. I thought of the coincidence with Dennis being in a similar line of business but decided not to make any mention of it. A few minutes later I felt it was time that I should be going. I got up ready to make my leave and then remembered the gift I had bought and originally planned to give to Rex at the club. I fumbled in my bag till I found it and then feeling slightly embarrassed handed it over. I watched as he took the little, gold brooch of dancer's shoes out of its box and turned it carefully in the early light that was starting to come in through the nets. His face radiated sheer delight as he held it delicately in his fingertips.

'Divine, absolutely divine.' His voice although warm now sounded very tired. 'You've salvaged my birthday, thank you for this'.

'My pleasure, Rex', I told him.

I felt relieved that my forgetting of his present till now had been a salvation. On leaving the block of flats, my thoughts were mixed with the night's activities as I headed for home, driving along the still quiet, desolate back streets of North London.

After that night Rex and I never had the same closeness. We spoke but we never really talked in depth. It was just the same old banter and theatre chat that now passed between us with the events of his birthday fading into the murkiness of the past along with all the other incidents that are thrown away back to the inner depths of one's mind. His wit remained, having lost none of its edge for, in actual fact, it seemed sharper which was no surprise to me knowing only too well that it could inevitably be used as a cover-up.

I only went back to the Pink Room a couple of times after that, having decided that it was no longer me, finding since the night of the birthday party that the place somehow left an unpleasant taste in my mouth, and that a kind of tackiness seemed to prevail which earlier I had not detected. As for the show, I stayed to the end of my year's contract and then left. Out of everyone there I only kept in touch with Joy for a couple of years afterwards until she decided to move back to Wales to become a singing teacher. As for the rest of them, I heard that some went on to appear in other shows and that quite a few had gone off in various directions, in and out of the business. Then one Saturday I ran into Alain in Tottenham Court Road on his way to a dance class and it was he who told me that Rex had stayed with the show till the bitter end, being one of only a handful of the original performers to do so and that since then no one had seen him or heard what he was doing.

I myself became the proverbial jobbing actress, with a succession of temporary office jobs in between. I was so thankful that I had learnt to type and, later on, acquired training on computers, for I was to find that this ability fortunately secured me lots of secretarial work and managed to keep the fear of the wolf well away from my door.

During these, the last years that I lived in London before moving out to live in Hampshire I moved only once more, finding myself through circumstances in a garden flat still north of the river, only a few miles from the city centre. The area's colourful and thriving market had been swapped with the shadow of a large skyscraper building that served the community with all its related problems concerning benefits, tax and insurance, and any other claims that people on a low income or finding themselves without a job might need to frequent. One freezing-cold, February morning, I approached this giant of a building to make an enquiry regarding my income tax return and saw the familiar snakelike line of people who always queued up early to wait for its doors to open. Just before joining it I happened to notice the person at the front of the queue, and it shocked me in disbelief. For, older by at least fifteen years or possibly more, there standing huddled by the locked doors was Rex Morris. I walked along slowly to take my place at the back of the line where, because of its reptilian curvature, I could observe him. He was wearing a grey flecked overcoat, and a hat that looked to me very much like a homburg. He still had a moustache, though it too resembled the coat he was wearing being flecked with grey, and any hair was well hidden away under his hat.

Suddenly with a jolt I was pushed forward as the queue started to move towards the now unlocking doors. Making my way through to the section that I needed, I wondered to what part Rex might be going. I wanted to observe him like a bystander watching from the sidelines. My wish was easily granted as, because he had been at the front of the queue, he was one of the first to get to a seat facing the bullet-proof glass window from where the office staff dealt with members of the public which was exactly the same place that I too was approaching. The mass of people had thinned out now due to the fact that the benefits office had segmented-off areas appertaining to whatever was relevant to them, with this part of a larger room smaller by comparison to the rest. Although due to the overall design of the place and the poorly partitioned walls, without even trying you could hear everything that each and every one of us was saying at the counter. Privacy has its price and this place had none and, even though my claim was only regarding correct completion of a tax return, I sensed only too well the overall air of despair and depression that hung around, as I had from time to time been signing on here for unemployment benefit, so knew the feelings and attitudes that made most people feel like second-class citizens.

I hesitated before taking a seat only four rows from the front, watching as Rex went to the first available window. I felt like a voyeur unable to stop myself from craning my neck trying to see what was going on behind the screen and then I heard Rex's unmistakable voice.

'What do you mean I can't continue to sign on anymore?' he bellowed at the young man behind the screen.

The assistant was obviously new to the job and said something and got up and disappeared to the back, the typical bolt that they usually did when they were not yet fully trained up or when, even with the presence of the screen, they felt that tempers were getting frayed.

While Rex sat there waiting, I could now see his face quite clearly. It had lost the healthy glow that I once remembered and looked perversely pallid, and his eyes, that had always had sparkle, were sunken in their sockets surrounded by heavy lines and creases. The assistant didn't return, instead a woman who looked from her appearance like she might be someone in charge, a manageress or something of the kind came and sat in front of the screen and leant towards it slightly as she spoke.

I saw Rex's back stiffen and then he raised himself up fully as he got up from his chair.

'Pension!' he spat his disgust as he said the word.

'Retirement pension!' This time he spoke the words with pure venom in his voice.

'I'm not a pensioner. I'm a dancer, a boy dancer that's what I am. I'm the oldest boy dancer in the business', he said standing up proudly.

I sat riveted to my seat as I watched Rex walk defiantly out of the building and felt relieved that I had luckily blended into the background along with all the others who were sitting there.

I didn't get to sort out my enquiry that day, for a few minutes after Rex had made his grand exit, I too got up and left, as I was unable to sit there any more waiting for my name to be called. I knew that it wasn't cowardice that had kept me from going after Rex, it was from a sense of pity for what he had become, from what the business had done to him. I never saw him again in all the time that I lived in the area and put his memory into a compartment in my mind filed under the heading of 'Boy Dancer'.

The All Too Perfect Teddy Bear

I was driving back from shopping one morning when I set eyes on the bear. It was being carried along on the pavement, almost engulfing the person transporting it. As I glanced over I instantly recognised the face behind the furry head, it was Brenda, a slightly eccentric young woman whom I knew, so the sight of her carrying an enormous teddy bear didn't surprise me one bit. I wound down the window and called over to her offering her a lift.

'Where on earth did you get that from?' I asked as she put the bear on the rear seat and fastened the safety belt securely round him, as if it was the most natural thing in the world to do.

'Found him on a tip,' she said excitedly.

I looked round studying him closely.

'But he looks brand new,' I replied, hardly believing my eyes at the sight of such a gorgeous cuddly toy being discarded.

'I know, can't understand why anyone would want to dump him. Must have been a spoilt kid with too many toys,' Brenda answered.

I didn't say anything more on the subject and pulling up at her flat I helped her get him out of the back of my car. When I got home, I went to get my bag out from off the back seat and noticed some small fragments of glass from where the bear had been sitting. They must have ended up in the fur from where Brenda had found him, I thought to myself as I carefully picked them off one by one till there were none left.

The following afternoon as I drove back from the post office, I was suddenly startled to hear a voice speak to me.

'What have you done with Ferdinand?'

I pulled the car over and turned towards the back seat to see a pretty little child, a girl of no more than six sitting upright in the same place that the bear had been the day before.

'Do you mean the teddy bear?' I said, surprised that I had left the car unlocked, for it meant she must have slipped in unnoticed.

'Yes, I need him to get to sleep,' she said softly.

I told her where her bear was and promised tomorrow I'd go and retrieve it for her, before dropping her off outside her house which was down a long road by a pedestrian crossing.

I thought nothing more about the incident until the following day when I went round to see Brenda who told me that she had taken the bear back to the tip because she had heard that it had previously come from the wreckage of a car crash, in which a little girl and her father had been killed outright. Apparently, it had happened directly outside their house, which was not that far away from here, at the bottom of a long road right next to a pedestrian crossing.

The Serving Hatch

They had lived with the hole in the wall for over a year now, ever since they had moved into the house, often promising themselves that they would get it fixed, but because there was still so much to do that was of greater importance, it had ended up very low down as a priority on the 'things we must do' list. Until that is certain circumstances started to force the issue, or more precisely the repeated antics caused by Charlie, their well-loved, attention- seeking, ginger tomcat.

Mark and Natalie had found their perfect house, after fortunately being able to sell their own places quite quickly when they had made the decision to move in together. Mark had been divorced for just over six years, but Natalie had never been married and except for one long relationship way back in her past, up until meeting Mark she had lived on her own for quite some time. Well, not exactly on her own, as she had Charlie, or they had each other as Natalie always used to tell people. Natalie was very fond of him, in fact she totally adored him. As a tiny kitten, he had been found living rough on a refuse dump near a disused railway station, and luckily been taken to the local animal shelter where he was nursed back to health. Natalie cried when she first saw him; she was a childless woman who, due to health problems, had undergone a hysterectomy in her early thirties, and when she had held the little warm creature close in her arms a few weeks after her operation, she knew that at last she had found something to love and care for. Because she was at that time still recuperating, she was at her flat all day, so for the first few months of Charlie's life she and he were inseparable. Natalie always claimed that this was the reason for the closeness between them, and then when she got better and returned to the office where she worked as a secretary, he had reluctantly had to get used to seeing her only of an evening and at weekends. He tolerated this arrangement, because

Natalie always made such a fuss of him on her return, and also because she brought home nice things for him to eat like raw liver and fresh prawns. Yes, Charlie had it made, he was thoroughly spoilt and like most felines in his position wouldn't want this workable arrangement to change, and for a good few years it didn't, until that is Mark appeared on the scene.

Natalie had met Mark through one of the usual ways that people meet, in the office. He had gone to Prescott's, the company where she worked, to organize and set up staff training in new software packages. Mark ran his own small computer training company and was starting to get a good return for all his hard efforts and determination in the field. More importantly, it was growing nicely, and he was just starting to expand. He and Natalie got on so well from their first meeting, and after a lunchtime drink two days later, started to meet up after Mark had completed his business at the company and very quickly were seen regularly going out together. Naturally Natalie had told Mark all about Charlie and was relieved to hear that although he didn't have any pets of his own, he liked animals, and more importantly he liked cats. Charlie didn't like Mark. Not at that first meeting or for that matter on the many occasions that Mark had started to come round to the flat, his domain, his home.

'What is that noise you're making?' asked Natalie looking down at the small, furry feline one evening just as Mark was hanging up his coat.

'Sounds like he's snorting if you ask me,' replied Mark.

'That's strange, he's never done that before,' Natalie told him, leaning down to stroke her companion. 'Are you alright my ginger genie,' she said calling him by his pet name, 'come on, let's give you something nice to eat.' And as she went out into the kitchen Charlie came running up behind following closely at her heels.

'I don't think he likes me you know,' said Mark while Charlie was happily chomping away at the carefully chopped-up pieces of liver that had been placed in his bowl on the plastic cat mat.

'Oh, don't be so ridiculous, you silly thing you,' Natalie answered pulling Mark towards her, and putting her arms around his neck.

'What about when we sit on the sofa together, he always jumps up and tries to push me away.'

'He just needs time to get used to you that's all.'

She kissed Mark gently. 'Come on let's sit down,' she said trying to pacify him.

They went over to the sofa and cuddled up closely to one another. Within seconds Charlie appeared, having left the last of his liver, and had as Mark said he would, jumped up and was now trying to force himself in between the two of them.

'What did I say?' Mark said looking over at Natalie, as the extremely persistent Charlie pushed his body further into the wedge he had made in between the two of them. Suddenly Natalie got hold of the irritant and carried him out into the kitchen.

'You've brought it on yourself,' she told him before firmly closing the door. Charlie was having none of this and started to meow incessantly and even when Natalie had gone back into the lounge to put some music on the pitiful sounds of emotional blackmail emitting from the crafty creature could still be heard.

'I'm not going to let him get his own way this time,' Natalie informed Mark as she sat down again. 'Anyway, he's bound to stop it in a minute.'

But Charlie didn't stop, not even when the music was turned up to try and drown him out. In the end the racket he was making got too much to bear, and he was let into the room again, only this time when he inevitably jumped up on the sofa, it was not to come between them, it was to sit himself comfortably down on Mark's lap. Surprisingly, he curled himself up, tail tucked under him and went quietly to sleep.

And so Charlie started to become quite attached to Mark, almost it seemed as if he was getting his own back on Natalie for introducing him to their cosy arrangement in the first place. Natalie didn't mind that much, after all she still gave him cuddles which of course being a cat he lapped up, but she herself now had a different kind of affection with Mark, and anyway she was pleased that the ginger cat had finally accepted him, and also because she had other things to concern herself with now, mainly the new house that they were all going to move into, the one that had just been agreed on.

***

'We really must do something about that carpet in the dining room,' said Mark one evening.

'Before that we need to do something about that hole,' Natalie told him and indicated over to the wall.

'It's not a hole, it's a serving hatch,' replied Mark reaching down to tie his shoelace.

'It would be if it had some sort of door on it. Besides, if we get a carpet, we'll have to get it done, we can't have Charlie going in there not with a new carpet.'

Charlie liked the old carpet, the old shag pile that the previous owners had left, and he liked the hole, or hatch as Mark called it. It was just at the right level for him to comfortably jump down into the dining room from the kitchen. He liked it in there, it was a great place for a cat to sleep, especially when he had returned from hunting his prey, which he always brought back and placed on the dining room carpet a yard or two from the hole.

'I'm fed up with for ever clearing up the mess in that room, there are still feathers from last week floating around. I thought I'd got them all and then I notice a few more,' said Natalie.

'Well, I don't like doing it either, so we'd better get someone round to put a door on. It shouldn't cost much, I mean it's only a small hatch,' said Mark picking up his briefcase, 'will you ring up someone?' he added.

Natalie arranged for two carpenters, and to be on the safe side, an odd-job man, to come round to give a quote and on the following Saturday the first one arrived to give his opinion.

'Sorry missus, I don't like cats, allergic to 'em you see,' said the man in the white overalls making for the door as soon as he saw Charlie's head appear through the cat flap.

'Well I only wish you'd put that in your advert, Mr. Mullins,' replied Natalie, escorting him out.

'He was rather quick,' said Mark as he came out of the bathroom. 'What did he have to say?'

'Not much, other than he was allergic to cats.'

'Oh,' Mark sighed, 'Not to worry, we've another two coming.'

Kevin Payne was next, and from his advert he seemed to come across as a chippie that could turn his hand to almost anything. He even brought a small photo album with pictures of some of the jobs he had done, most of them being in the line of made-to-measure bookcases. Mark wondered if he was touting for other work as he really didn't seem to be that interested in the serving hatch at all and was being somewhat persistent in inquiring about what other jobs they might have in mind. Also, he said that he had a 'friend' who did a nice little line in microwave ovens if they were interested. Mark said it was only the hatch that they had in mind today, and asked if it was possible for Kevin to give them the quote there and then, as they were in a hurry to get it done.

Kevin started to measure up the empty space of the serving hatch, oblivious to Charlie's watchful eyes looking on at the proceedings from where he was surveying the scene, on top of the boiler, one of his favourite haunts.

'Hundred,' he said reeling his tape back up.

'Is that all,' Mark replied somewhat sarcastically.

'It's a tricky thing to make and there's the wood as well. Believe me, it's not an easy thing to just knock up.'

Neither Mark nor Natalie seemed that convinced.

‘We’ll have a think about it and let you know if we want you to do the job,’ Mark told him, wishing Kevin would hurry up and get in his van the one with ‘K. Payne, The Chippie Chappy’ on the side, and go.

‘Don’t leave it too long, I’ve got a lot on and there’s plenty more people wanting jobs done’.

‘So, you won’t be that bothered if you don’t do our hatch then?’ Mark replied whilst walking out of the kitchen into the hallway.

Kevin started to back down from his high horse. ‘Oh, don’t get me wrong, I’m not saying that I don’t want to do it’, he said quickly following Mark. ‘Look, maybe we can negotiate on the price, and what about one of those microwaves I was telling you about, very reasonable they are. You have one of them and I’ll take a bit off for knocking up the hatch door.’

‘We have your number Mr. Payne, thank you for coming,’ replied Mark, whose relief was more than self-evident when he closed the front door.

‘Two down, one to go,’ Natalie said with a long sigh, as she handed Mark a mug of hot tea. ‘Maybe we’ll be luckier with the odd-job man, Mr Tye.’

But Mr Tye didn’t show, or for that matter even telephone. Mrs Tye however did call the following day, to say that her husband had put his back out, climbing up a ladder, to get their cat Tyler out of the hawthorn bush in their front garden.

‘Oh, so he likes cats then,’ said a pleased Natalie, ‘Let’s hope Charlie will like him’.

‘I doubt very much if Charlie’s even going to clap eyes on him,’ Mark replied. ‘The doctor says Mr Tye has to rest up as much as possible and told him not to do anything that resembles work for at least two to three weeks.’

‘We could always do it ourselves, I suppose,’ said Natalie enthusiastically. ‘Come on let’s go over the road to the DIY shop and see what we can come up with. You never know we may be lucky and find just what we’re after.’

As luck would have it, they did find exactly what they needed, for in the shop was a very small cupboard door, and size wise it was the exact measurements they had written down. So, they bought it, along with some wood stain which once applied would finish the job off nicely.

They were so pleased with themselves, that they even went into Norris's carpet shop in the High Street and splashed out on ordering a new, short-cut, weave-wool carpet in a warm, peachy- pink tone. Mr. Norris said that the order wouldn't take very long as the supplier he used was very quick, and he reckoned that he would shortly be able to come round to fit it.

On returning home, Mark intended that he would make a start on the serving hatch door the following day, but like a lot of good intentions and possibly a long lunchtime drink at the Brown Bear with his friend Stuart, it didn't get started. In fact, for the next couple of weeks, both Mark and Natalie hit a high spot with work and also with pleasure. They didn't usually have much of a social life but suddenly that started to improve, and they found themselves rushing in and out from work to go straight out again. Charlie watched all this frenetic activity with his usual, catlike expression, his watchful eyes darting across at the both of them, the two people who at one time gave him so much affection and playtime, who now hardly bothered to even stroke him or call out his name when they came in, let alone give him longed-for, lap-time cuddles. He was not a happy cat and, when they had gone out again, he would jump through the 'hole' straight down into the corner of the dining room and curl up quietly going asleep on the comforting, familiar, old, shag-pile carpet.

'Friday afternoon,' Natalie said to Mark as she came into the lounge, 'Mr Norris has left us a message on the answerphone to say that he has the carpet in, and can come round and fit it for us.'

'Great. We can invite Tess and Stuart round on Saturday for a meal, it'll make a change to stay in for once.'

‘Don’t you think you should put the door on before then?’ said Natalie looking over at the hole in the wall of the dining room.

‘Saturday, I promise.’

He noticed Natalie’s expression and went over and put his arm round her shoulder, ‘It will get done this time, I mean it, don’t worry.’

‘It’s not you I’m worried about, it’s Charlie,’ Natalie replied looking over towards the cat flap.

‘But its ages since he’s brought any birds home, if that’s what’s bothering you. He’s most probably forgotten all about them by now,’ said Mark trying to reassure her.

On Thursday evening when they got home from work, Mark and Natalie cleared the dining room and set about removing the old carpet. After it was finally rolled up, they managed with some effort, to get it out and put it down by the side of the house. Mark covered it over with some plastic covering to keep it dry ready for being collected by the local Council. Natalie set about sweeping the floor of the room, while Charlie watched her, looking through the ‘hole’ from the worktop on the other side in the kitchen.

‘I’ve got a lovely surprise for you, ginger genie,’ said Natalie as she swept up the last, lingering particles of dust. She put the broom down and went over to where Charlie was sitting, his whole body framed in the square, empty space in the wall. Charlie stretched his head up towards Natalie’s face, the soft ginger fur of the feline felt delightful as she stroked under his chin with her fingertips, so reminiscent of the days long gone when they had spent so much time together. The cat purred with pure pleasure.

‘Wait here and I’ll go and get it for you.’

When Natalie returned, she walked into the kitchen and placed a small cat igloo on the kitchen floor.

‘There, isn’t that lovely, Charlie, much better than that old carpet. You have your own little house now.’

But Charlie didn't want his own 'little house' as Natalie had put it, he wanted the old shag pile, the carpet that was gone but not forgotten. That night he went out of his cat flap and stayed out all night. Mr Norris arrived as planned and fitted the new carpet the following afternoon, Natalie having taken time off to be home to let him in. The new carpet looked glorious; it was the latest fashion in the carpet trade apparently, according to the pamphlet that came with the manufacturers guarantee. And it had to be said that the colour really did suit the furniture and go extremely well with the decor. In fact, the whole room looked very nice indeed, through the eyes of a human.

'I hope Charlie's going to go into his igloo tonight,' said Natalie as she and Mark got into bed that night.

'Well, he'll have to eventually as I'm going to put that door on tomorrow morning, so he's only got tonight on the new carpet.'

But Charlie didn't spend the night on the carpet in the dining room. For the second time in succession he went out through his cat flap, kicking the side with one of his hind legs as he did so, making it close rather rapidly, creating a louder than average noise just as the lock closed and the flap snapped itself shut.

'He's not slept in his igloo again,' said Natalie sadly as she and Mark went downstairs into the kitchen the next morning.

'I expect he's been out again, you know cats are really nocturnal animals,' Mark told her as he walked over to the sink to fill the kettle.

'Yes, but that's only when they're out hunt... oh, my God, my God!' said Natalie covering her mouth with her hands to stop herself from screaming in disbelief. Through the serving hatch, her eyes focused on the scene that awaited them both in the dining room. Not just feathers, oh no, there was blood and entrails of a large blackbird, even though not much had been consumed. It had been left on what had been the new virgin carpet, which was now soiled and soaked in bloodstains. The culpable creature was evident, he lay there on his side in the corner of the room, looking every inch the satisfied hunter, ritualistically licking and washing himself, cleaning his fur of the last few frond-like feathers that had attached themselves to his coat during the kill. He was immersed in the scene he had created, to the horrified stares of Mark and Natalie.

'You beast, you vile creature! Look what you've done!' Mark shouted at him through the space in the wall that separated the three of them.

'No Mark, it's what *we've* done. Can't you see that?' replied Natalie.

Her voice alerted Charlie, who stopped washing himself and stood up, stretching his entire body as he did so. Gracefully he moved slowly over towards the serving hatch, stepping through the debris and broken bits of bird and jumped through the space into the kitchen and down onto the floor. Two still-stunned faces watched as he totally ignored both of them, walking over to his cat flap and going out, with the last thing to be seen going through it being the furry tip of his ginger tail.

The Donkey of Asinara

Gareth had hoped that this particular holiday would be more than a lift for Jenny. He was naturally under no illusions of a complete cure, knowing only too well by now that severe clinical depression was a hard nut to crack. Managing to alleviate the feelings of hopelessness that had dogged his wife for much of their marriage, was difficult at the best of times. So, a temporary respite by way of a pleasant summer holiday was the most that could possibly be expected.

They had first met nearly four years ago, when they were both working for the Opera House. He hadn't failed to notice her, who amongst the orchestra couldn't, for as the leading light of her generation of sopranos she was truly outstanding. Along with the gift of a unique talent, she radiated from the moment she walked out onto the stage. It therefore came as a complete shock to Gareth when he came across her late one afternoon howling like a dog in the corner of a deserted rehearsal room. Was this really the same sensational woman that he'd had the utmost pleasure in accompanying as second violinist?

Initially he was unsure of what to do. His reason for returning was to pick up his pocket diary that he had inadvertently left behind approximately an hour beforehand. So, the sight of Jenny crumpled up like a disused newspaper hugging herself tightly with her arms as she cried out to the rows of empty chairs was more than unsettling.

He could have discreetly slipped away, returning the following day when in all probability his diary would still be there, and the disturbing spectacle of this unhappy woman would be no more. Most people in his shoes would have done just that, for fear of intrusion leading to disclosure and possible involvement. But for Gareth this in itself was not an issue, for he was not the type to walk away from distress.

It took only a few minutes for Jenny to tell him what was making her so upset. Or more to the point, who. It was their charismatic Czech conductor who had not only broken her heart but also had enough influence in the opera company to ‘request’ another soprano for the next season. If that wasn’t bad enough, it transpired that the ‘requested’ soprano was also succumbing to his charisma in his rented house in Muswell Hill.

Gareth listened attentively to the flow of words coming from Jenny’s lips. He was astute enough to realise that it was better this way, for her to get it all out of her system, till there were no more angry words left to say and she was all spent. And after she had become calmer, her embarrassment took hold and she started to apologise. Reassurances, plus the offer of going for a coffee, cleverly diverted her attention from what had just gone before. Although it was to raise its head from time to time as a relationship started to form between the two of them, it disappeared in due course and faded quietly into the background. Partly because Jenny decided to leave the company on the advice of her agent and subsequently take on freelance work, performing with whatever opera company requested her appearance as its guest soprano. And there were plenty who did want her to sing for them, as sopranos of her calibre were a rarity. This was all well and good for a while, but such a rapid success meant that the amount of travelling involved started to spiral, and as demand for her increased, she had to spend more and more time away.

Surprisingly, Jenny and Gareth’s relationship did not suffer from these partings, in fact it helped to cement the bond between them even more. They married after less than a year to the delight of both families and colleagues in the opera world. They were both by now very much in love with one another, and each time he collected her from the airport when she returned from a trip abroad, they were both brimming with happiness at being once more together again.

Eventually it was the strain of this constant travel, by now coupled with the rigours of even more demanding operatic roles that lead to her inevitable breakdown. At first it manifested itself in that she was not able to manage some of the top notes in her register, and then she started to display some quite out-of- character behaviour, some of it rather erratic, and later there were volatile scenes happening off stage. She had never been a prima donna, so it was a complete surprise for those who had the misfortune to observe such a change in a person. The crash came more dramatically than anything she had ever played on stage; it was that fearsome. The physical exhaustion was like a huge wave of constant tiredness battering against her. She found she was hardly able to walk let alone capable of being able to think to function.

Many long, harrowing months of treatment followed. But in the end, it was the constant support and tireless patience of Gareth that was to aid Jenny's recovery. Unlike his wife, as a musician he was able to get a deputy in very easily to cover for the evenings he needed to be away from the orchestra to be her nurse. His understanding company manager, like so many of those who knew her, wanted Jenny to be well again, however long it would take. Which it did, along with it, its toll.

Although she got better and some would say over her breakdown, what was left was a changed woman. She functioned again, but the spirit that had been broken and pieced back together wasn't able to cope with life in the same way. The doctor had told Gareth that it could take time, although he couldn't be drawn as to how long that might be. He had also warned that things might never be the same again. The marked clinical depression and the inability to want to sing were now her legacy.

Of course, this meant that there was no question that she would be able to resume her career. She still had her voice, which Gareth heard on the odd occasion, early in the morning. Realising that she was not still sleeping beside him, he would get up and looking through the bedroom window he'd see her walking in the garden on her own, singing lightly to herself, though it was only a few bars at a time before she stopped.

He never mentioned that he had seen her. Nor did he argue when feelings of low self-esteem raised their ugly heads like a mythical gorgon, and she shouted at him using him like a punch-bag to vent her anger. Tears and hours of frustrated words of regrets for what had happened did nothing to dent his love for his wife.

Days out and holidays were fortunately a help in restoring a temporary balance to Jenny. She seemed to show a marked improvement and almost became like her former self, for a while at least. So, when Gareth suggested a holiday in Sardinia, she had been very keen to go. They were not going to be staying at a large resort on the island. Instead, after flying into Alghero, they had picked up their hire car and headed along the Coral Riviera towards the fishing village of Stintino. Tuna fishing, once the mainstay of the Stintinese, had now been replaced by tourists who usually stayed in holiday villages on the outskirts of town. But Gareth had chosen something quiet and secluded – a small, eight roomed hotel behind the main street with views from the top two floors out to sea. None of this was down to chance work. He had been here once before, as a young boy accompanying his father while he was doing research work into the seabirds that congregated in the area. They had stayed for part of the summer and for much of the time Gareth had been taken under the wing of the family who owned the hotel. It had been a memorable experience for a small boy, a happy time that he had stored away like a time capsule.

Twenty-five years on, Claudia and her husband Paulo were still there running their business. They welcomed him with genuine warmth, remarking on how he had turned into a fine young man. Jenny, though, pulled back behind Gareth showing the familiar signs of nervousness that she now displayed with strangers. At one time confidence would have run through her, and she would have introduced herself without any hesitation. Claudia took it to be shyness on Jenny's part and rushed over and hugged her like she would a daughter. After some more conversation, Paulo carried their luggage upstairs and showed them their room, which was at the very top of the hotel, the one requested by Gareth.

'It's hardly changed!' he exclaimed looking around at the simply furnished room. 'Just as I seem to remember it, though it has a bathroom en-suite now.'

He went over to the window and opened the shutters, and as he did so, Paulo slipped skilfully away and disappeared downstairs, leaving them to themselves.

'Jenny, look, look at the view,' he said turning back towards her, his hand hastily beckoning her over.

'Oh, it's beautiful, and just look at the colour of that sea,' she exclaimed in astonishment when she came over and saw it through her own eyes.

Gareth put his arm around his wife and the two of them looked out of the window together.

'It's incredible, I've never seen anything so blue, it's the colour of rich turquoise.'

Jenny's eyes gazed out at the intoxicating sea, with its swirling shades of blues and greens that mixed together making one of the finest palate of colours an artist could only ever dream of.

'Shall we go and see the village?' asked Gareth, diverting Jenny's gaze.

'I'd like that, yes, and then we can unpack later.'

The brooding cloud of depression had been temporarily discarded, and she picked up her straw hat ready to explore the town.

They went outside and walked through Stintino's colourful streets, often said to be similar to a North African village with their rich ochre-and-pink-shaded houses. Jenny pointed out the most interesting ones as they passed by before stumbling on a back-street bar in which they had long glasses of lemonade to quench their thirsts.

Returning to the hotel, Claudia asked them if they would like to join her and Paulo for dinner that evening. Jenny felt nervous by the invitation, but so as not to disappoint Gareth she agreed to go.

'If you'd rather not, I can always ring down and say that you're tired after the journey,' said Gareth when they were back in their room, seeing and knowing too well that she was starting to feel unsure of herself.

'No, no, it's alright really. I'll be fine,' she said, her voice sounding shaky.

'They are lovely people and they like you, especially Claudia, I can tell,' he said to reassure her.

'You're just saying that, Gareth.'

'Have I ever lied to you?'

He cupped her exquisite face in his hands and gently kissed her.

Later that evening after an enjoyable dinner in Claudia's kitchen, nicely rounded off by a glass of Mirto, the local digestive, Gareth started to reminisce about his previous stay with his father. Although it was such a long time ago, he remembered much about that particular summer, and especially his time spent on the nearby island of Asinara.

Jenny listened to her husband's description intently. It was a pocket of Gareth's life that he hadn't spoken about in so much detail before. Yes, she did know that he had been to Sardinia as a child, but until they had arrived that was all she really knew. Unknown to her because of her illness, which had consumed them both, he had chosen to focus his attention solely on her, and his precious boyhood memories were not touched upon. But now he talked freely about them and 'Isola di Asinara', and its wildlife; the various seabirds his late father had studied, the wild boars, and the rare species of albino donkey, for which Asinara was known throughout the world.

Later that week they made the short journey by sea over to Asinara by way of one of the 'boat-buses', which go back and forth daily, taking visitors and various professionals in the fields of zoology or naturalism to its shores.

Paulo had asked to accompany them on their visit. For it was he who used to take Gareth over to watch his father at his work, observing and classifying seabirds. By now he was familiar to Jenny and she accepted him with ease to join them. She heard him tell the various tales about Asinara, that it had been dedicated to Hercules, and at one time even had a hermit. But it was the story of the albino donkeys that fascinated Jenny. Paulo told her that not only were they a rarity, and the only ones in the entire world, but because of their purity by way of their whiteness, they were attributed to possess special healing powers.

'What sort of healing do they do?' Jenny asked.

'Whatever is required of them,' said Paulo, helping her from the boat and onto the landing deck.

They proceeded along the shoreline and started to head away from the rest of the passengers, following an unmarked dirt track that would only have been noticeable to extremely observant eyes. Paulo led them along this path, and their footsteps retraced those that the young Gareth had first made so many summers ago. Screeching gulls flew over their heads out towards the sea, but they were not heading towards the cliffs, they were walking inwards to where the donkeys took their sanctuary.

The place that they came to was near to some shaded rocks where the gentle, snow-white creatures protected themselves away from the sun's rays. Some of them could be seen sleeping, occasionally shaking an ear to distract passing flies. Paulo found a spot for them to sit down and he laid out a blanket and opened a picnic basket he had brought. Claudia had made up a packed lunch for them which they now ate, surrounded by the donkeys who didn't seem to mind their presence and continued to doze.

But Jenny felt she needed to get closer to them, and without speaking to either Gareth or Paulo she got up and walked towards one of the rocks.

Paulo reached over and put his hand on Gareth's arm to stop him from intervening and shook his head.

'No, it is best to leave her. Do not worry, they will not harm.'

Jenny slowly walked towards one of the sleeping animals, and as she approached it raised its head and looked up at her. Carefully she knelt down beside the creature and almost instinctively a furry head was placed on her lap. Jenny began to stroke the little albino donkey, talking to it softly, feeling the comforting warmth that was radiating from under its coarse coat, while the donkey's eyelids outlined by a delicate pinkish hue once again closed as it returned to a contented slumber. As Gareth and Paulo continued to watch the moving encounter from where they were sitting, a faint lullaby started to be heard. And as he listened to the extraordinary sound of his wife's singing, Gareth knew that this time she didn't intend to stop.

The Leather Jerkin

It was one of those letters that only a few people ever receive, the type of which once their contents have unfolded are almost certain to bring apprehension in their wake.

Andrew replaced the letter back into its envelope and placed it carefully in his briefcase. He would ring the solicitor's once he had had a chance to talk to Kate. There was no rush, a day or two would be acceptable. He loosened his tie and crossed over to the fridge and took out a beer. Strange, he thought to himself as he started to pour his drink, how something like that can turn up out of the blue on the doormat. It had taken them two months, not that long really for tracing the only surviving son and relative of a deceased father. He placed the rim of the glass to his lips and let the cold liquid run easily down his throat. The cool sensation of the welcoming beer soothed his senses as he started to gather his thoughts. Twenty-eight years had elapsed since the day he remembered last setting eyes on his father. In his mind he started to delve backwards into his childhood, trying to recall anything he could of that time, or the man whom his mother had walked out on. Later on when he was quite a few years older, he had accepted what was said to him, that his parents had just not got on anymore and that at the time his mother had thought it was for the best for Andrew and her to leave. Although he became in effect the only child of a one-parent family, it didn't hinder him as he and his mother had moved in with his grandparents and Andrew had spent the happiest of childhoods surrounded by immediate family who adored him. This satisfactory arrangement enabled Andrew's mother Margaret to continue with her secure job working in the accounts department of a large ship-broking company. So, the absence of Andrew's father was of no consequence to the boy, for his grandfather took him under his wing and he never once felt deprived of the missing parent.

'Hello Andy,' said Kate lively as she entered the kitchen laden down with bags of shopping.

Andrew rushed over to help his girlfriend, quickly taking the heaviest looking plastic carrier bag from her.

'God, what have you got in there, it weighs a ton,' he remarked as he lifted the bag up to the worktop.

'Just potatoes and some goodies for our meal tonight.'

'Um, looks interesting,' said Andrew taking out the bag's contents. 'Wow, chocolate-almond cheesecake, you spoil me.'

He moved over to Kate and planted a delicate kiss on her cheek.

'It's not all for you, you know,' she said smiling affectionately back at him.

But of course the fact that Kate knew it was one of Andrew's favourite desserts, one that she could only get from the Italian Delicatessen at the bottom of the High Street, had totally influenced her decision to buy the cheesecake. It had meant an extra walk from the station to get to the shop, but Kate didn't mind. She indulged him, and he likewise did the same for her whenever the opportunity arose.

They had initially met through Kate's brother Giles, who had turned up on his sister's doorstep one evening after losing his key. Kate had kept a couple of spares just in case her brother lost his, as he was apt to do on more than one occasion after a night out with his work colleagues. They only lived a short walking distance from one another in flats near the Broadway, which was very fortunate for Giles. By way of an apology he invited her round the following weekend for one of his famous spaghetti western weekenders, where the flat would almost heave under the amount of spaghetti, Clint Eastwood movies and people it was expected to accommodate. Kate was not that fussed about the films, but the food and the people were generally a good mix, so she accepted. That was the weekend where she met Andrew. He occupied the flat below, having not that long moved in, so

Giles had the good sense to invite him just in case things got a bit out of hand in the noise department which they invariably did at one of his weekenders. Neither Kate nor Andrew saw much of Clint Eastwood that weekend. They were too busy chatting in Andrew's garden below with a chilled glass of Chardonnay, and a couple of plates of spaghetti, which they had sneaked out and taken downstairs with them. And now less than eighteen months later they were making the final arrangements for their wedding. Kate had for the time being decided to rent out her flat and moved in with Andrew as his was the larger of the two. But the grand plan was to eventually sell them both and move to a house, somewhere with more greenery, though neither of them could quite make up their minds where that somewhere was going to be, and with prices the way they were at the moment it was much easier and more sensible to stay put for the time being.

'That was a delicious meal,' said Andrew wiping away a small trace of chocolatey almond flakes from the corner of his mouth.

'Yes, and Silvano's cheesecake gets better each time,' replied Kate as she got up and started clearing the plates.

'Coffee?'

'Great,' he answered picking up the cream jug before going over to help her make it.

Although Andrew had decided that he wanted to tell Kate about the contents of the letter, he had deliberately put it on hold during their evening meal. He knew full well that there would be the inevitable questions, the answers to which he didn't have. But to delay telling her now at this juncture, well, maybe that wouldn't be such a good idea either he thought to himself. No, much better to come clean, get it all out in the open so to speak. Well, as much as he could at any rate.

'Anything you want to watch on TV tonight?' said Kate opening the fridge door to get the milk for the coffee.

'Err no, I don't think so,' he replied scratching around for a reply.

'Andy, are you alright, you seem a bit distant.'

'Something came up, I mean came in the post today,' he answered trying to jumble the right words together. 'Look, let's sit down shall we, and if the phone goes let's leave it to go onto the answerphone, eh?'

'OK,' said Kate, studying her fiancé's face looking for clues as to what he might be about to tell her.

She followed him into the lounge with the coffee and sat down not on the sofa, as she would usually do, sitting up close right next to him, but in the chair that had its back towards the window.

'I received a letter today, from a firm of solicitors', he paused prudently before continuing, 'they wrote to tell me that my father had died.'

'Oh, Andy I'm sorry. But how did they find you?'

'Well, there are ways, and I suppose agencies for that sort of thing. Anyway, they want me to contact them regarding sorting out his house and possessions.'

'It must be an awful shock,' said Kate, adding, 'Especially as you never knew him.'

Andrew looked away for an instant feeling traitorous.

'That's where you're wrong, Kate, I did, well for a short time as a small child at any rate.'

'But I thought you told me that your mother left your father just after you were born,' Kate replied, wondering why on earth this part of Andrew's early life had been omitted.

'That's not exactly true. I, we, lived together as a family until I was round about six, possibly seven. Look it doesn't really matter does it,' he said, starting to get agitated.

'I suppose you didn't want to rake up the past, was that the reason you didn't tell me?' Kate inquired thinking she was entering shaky ground.

'No, it wasn't that. It was because, well, I've always thought that my childhood was so perfect and normal. I honestly can't remember a lot about him, my dad that is. My grandfather, yes, as I told you he was the one I always looked upon like a father.'

Kate got up from her chair and went and sat next to her fiancé on the sofa, sensing that her immediate closeness would be appreciated. She sat and listened as Andrew started to talk about his happy childhood, from which Kate could now clearly see had been well constructed to shield him away from the root cause of his parents' broken marriage. As she continued listening to his reminiscences, she started to have the oddest feeling that there was something more than not getting on together behind his mother's decision for leaving Andrew's father. Even when Andrew had matured there was no hint of any discussion, a coming-of-age explanation of the reasons behind her previous actions. It was as if his mother had drawn a heavy veil over her distant marriage and her expectations for Andrew to do the same for his early childhood had been totally complied with.

'Anyway, tomorrow I'll ring the solicitors and make an appointment to see their Mr Hillier', said Andrew when he had finally dispensed with his recollections. 'I'm sure he will be able to enlighten me.'

Kate realised it was best to leave things as they were for the time being. No point in any more questions she thought to herself, there would be more clarification once Andrew had been to the solicitors, of that she was certain.

On the Tuesday morning of the following week, Andrew arrived a good fifteen minutes early for his 10 o' clock appointment with Mr Gerald Hillier of Brace & Hillier, Solicitors. Their offices were situated in not unfamiliar territory for Andrew, a stone's throw from Turnpike Lane. This was the area that he knew well, as both his mother and grandmother used to do all their shopping there. His grandparents' house had only been a short walking distance from all their needs, which were met in the busy local shops nearby. It had always been a working-class district, and although many of the outlets had changed hands, overall it still displayed a familiarity. Brace & Hillier's offices were tucked tightly in between a dry cleaners on one side, and a kebab shop on the other. An old, brown, finger-worn, wooden door opened almost immediately onto a sheer flight of stairs that were each covered by remnants of old, faded-out, grey lino. As Andrew ascended, he noticed a thin, black arrow pointing along a corridor at the top of the stairs ushering clients towards a reception area of sorts, in which sat a somewhat sedate middle-aged woman behind a rather ancient looking PC, and perched strategically in front of the computer was her name, 'Miss Pym' displayed in gold lettering on a neat plastic strip.

'Mr Wilson?' she enquired vacantly, looking over the rim of her glasses.

'Yes, tis' I,' replied Andrew rather cheerily, deliberately trying to lighten up the austere atmosphere in the reception area.

'Theatrical, are you?' the expression on Miss Pym's face started to warm. 'Oh, I do love anything to do with the theatre, I find it all so exciting.'

'I'm sorry to disappoint you, but I'm nothing to do with the theatre, actually I'm a chiropodist.'

'Oh, pity,' she said returning her face to its previous demeanour. 'But you did sound very convincing, I can usually tell if someone has ability.'

'Mr Wilson do come through,' the booming voice of Gerald Hillier beckoned.

Andrew turned to see a commanding and rather overweight figure in a well-cut, worsted suit loitering in the doorway of the office nearby.

'You'll have to excuse our Miss Pym, she does get rather carried away sometimes', he said as he closed the door behind them, while gesturing to Andrew where to sit down. 'Anything to do with acting and she's off. But she's a real treasure, knows where everything's kept, marvellous person really.'

Andrew smiled agreeably.

'Now, to get down to business,' said Gerald Hillier as he seated himself comfortably behind his Churchillian-looking desk.

'I have in my possession the legal papers relating to the estate of your late father Charles Wilson.' He glanced down at a buff-coloured folder in front of him and turned the first page. 'I trust that you have brought with you the necessary certification for proof of your identity?'

Andrew leaned over as best he could and passed his birth certificate and driving licence across to the solicitor.

'Yes, well that all looks in order,' said the solicitor after carefully studying them. 'I'll get Miss Pym to make some copies for our files if that's alright with you,' he added.

Andrew nodded whilst Gerald Hillier swiftly called his secretary over the internal intercom to collect the documents. She appeared almost as soon as the switch on the intercom had been clicked back into place by one of his stubby fingers. Obediently she took the items handed to her and whisked them away to make the desired number of copies.

During the brief interlude before her return, the solicitor continued.

'As you said in your telephone call last week, you hadn't seen or even heard from your father for a great many years.'

'That's correct, since my early childhood when I was round about seven years old.'

'And you have no other close relatives now living?' replied Gerard Hillier.

'No, my grandparents passed away in quick succession of one another when I was in my early twenties and then my mother...,' Andrew hesitated now remembering back to something that had touched him deeply, '...my mother died three years ago, of cancer.'

Gerald Hillier studied the younger man's face, seeing the lasting impression the finality of a mother's death can have on an only son.

At that point Miss Pym conveniently gave the briefest of taps on the office door and after being asked to enter, carefully placed the documents and photocopying on Gerald Hillier's desk and discretely returned to her own area outside in reception.

'This must all be very distressing for you.' Gerald Hillier spoke in tones of well-perfected professional sympathy. 'Would you like a cup of coffee?'

Andrew shook his head in a polite gesture of refusal before continuing.

The solicitor studied Andrew's face out of inquisitiveness for any signs of anticipated greed for what may or may not be in store for him. None was showing, except the possibility of some tenseness, which under the circumstances could quite rightly be understood.

'Well I expect that you're wondering what my part is in this matter,' said Gerald Hillier as he began to put Andrew in the picture. 'I was instructed by the local council to deal with your late father's estate and to locate any next of kin. They had been informed of his death by the police.' He paused for a second before continuing. 'It appears that he died of natural causes, heart failure to be precise, and was not found for several days, hence the police involvement. A neighbour rang them to say that she hadn't seen your father going in or out for some time, she also told them that he lived a very solitary existence and didn't have any callers except for the milkman when he needed paying.'

'No one?' Andrew asked in astonishment, hardly comprehending the notion, 'Surely there must have been someone.'

'Apparently not, and this,' said Gerald Hillier passing a page from the folder across the desk to Andrew, 'was where he was living.'

'That was our old address,' Andrew told him, gazing down at the information on the sheet of paper; 14 Prentice Street, South Tottenham N15.

'Legally it's all yours now, along with the contents, which are a few pieces of furniture, and the total sum of £79 in cash that was found in the property, in a biscuit tin on the top of a sideboard I believe.' Gerald Hillier paused before taking his time continuing, 'It appears that there was nothing else of personal value except for this.' He handed Andrew a cheap wristwatch with a visible crack etched across its glass.

After putting his signature to a variety of legal documents, Andrew walked out of the offices of Brace and Hillier with a brown envelope in which had his father's wristwatch, the £79 and only one door key, which had previously laid next to the rusting biscuit tin on the sideboard. A mixture of bewilderment and uncertainty about what had led to the solitary existence of his father now filled his head. He walked determinedly down the street, trying to piece it all together, but he couldn't. On the way back to the station he was relieved to find a bread shop that served hot drinks and pastries at the back, so he went in and sat down and ordered a tea and a Danish pastry. He didn't usually eat anything until lunchtime, but the recent revelations had left him empty, though he wasn't sure that sustenance would relieve the hollow sensation that he was feeling inside. He took the envelope from his briefcase and prised open the flap holding the contents securely inside. It was one of those universal self-seal type of envelopes, the ones that if only just sealed by someone with a light touch come apart. Carefully he put his hand inside and felt around, and then withdrew it once he had hold of the door key. He held it up in front of him, turning it round, eyeing the smoothness and wear from years of the key being placed into the lock of the door that had been the house that Andrew had such vague memories about. Only now was his mind starting to probe. He clutched the metal tightly, not for comfort but for solidity of touch, from something that would take him back to a closed past he never dreamed that he would revisit. Nor even at this moment in time had any particular desire to, if the truth were known. He placed the key back into the envelope, hearing it drop to the bottom as he folded the top over in two, before putting it into his briefcase. He had on this occasion no intention of going to the house, for not only did he have a couple of challenging patients to see back at the practice, but he wanted to leave himself with plenty of time to digest whatever the house and its locked-up memories might hold in store.

Later on, in the early evening, Andrew stood on the steps outside his flat. He took his own door key out from his pocket and before placing it in the lock, turned it around in his fingers, just as he had done previously with the unfamiliar key that had been waiting for him in the offices of Brace and Hillier. It was the first time that he had ever done such a thing and there was the sense of familiarity, coupled with belonging that he felt comforted by such an innocent act. He placed the key in the lock and felt it turn with ease as it opened and he was let in. Tonight, Kate had arrived back earlier than Andrew and from the look and smell of things was in the process of making a stir fry.

'Do you want me to get you a beer?' she enquired after greeting him fondly.

'No, I'll think I'll just have some mineral water,' he answered before going into the bedroom to change. He wasn't looking forward to telling her of the outcome of his visit to the solicitors that morning. Knowing her as he did, he knew that she was deliberately not going to broach the subject herself, which although admirable, was also somewhat annoying to Andrew. It made him feel uneasy, as until he himself decided to bring it up, there would be tension between them of unspoken business. He went to the bathroom and had a wash down, letting the excess water from his facecloth run down the back of his neck, dripping down below his shoulders. He reached for his towel on the warm heated rail and patted himself dry.

'It's almost ready!' he heard Kate call out as he went back into the bedroom to get dressed, before returning to the kitchen.

They both ate slowly as Andrew started to give an account of his meeting with Gerald Hillier.

'How very, very sad,' said Kate when Andrew told her that his father had apparently not had any visitors, and to all intents and purposes had died friendless.

'I can't understand it either, until I go there I don't think I'll find any answers.'

'Maybe there aren't any, maybe he was just a loner.'

Andrew declined to reply and put down his fork indicating that he had finished with his meal, although he hadn't eaten very much. Kate's cooking was always first-rate, but the topic of conversation this evening didn't sit very well with a chicken stir fry. In his mind he couldn't accept Kate's theory, it just didn't stack up for him.

'Would you like to go alone, Andy?' Kate asked giving Andrew the option.

'Not especially, I was hoping that you would come with me.'

'Of course I will. Is it somewhere in London?' Kate enquired looking interested.

'Yes, in actual fact it's in South Tottenham, Prentice Street,' he said sheepishly.

'What!' Kate shouted, her voice immediately changing its tone. 'South Tottenham. I don't believe it, you lived in Prentice Street and you never told me.' She said now raising her voice in anger.

'Please calm down Kate, I know it was stupid of me, but I thought that it was incidental. Besides as I told you I only lived there for a few of my early years, I didn't think it was important.'

He went over to put an arm round her but she brushed him away.

'Not to you maybe, but to me, yes.'

She started to pace around the room in agitation.

'First you conceal from me that you didn't know your father, and then it comes to light that not only did you live with him, but it was in the same area as I was brought up, and if you hadn't received that solicitor's letter you wouldn't have told me! What more are you hiding from me, Andy?' she said, looking at her fiancée with unfamiliar, accusatory eyes.

Andrew didn't have any answers. The veil that he had learnt from his mother to draw over his early years had now been pulled off and firmly ripped to shreds. But Kate's reaction, her dramatic outburst so out of character for her, gave him the notion that he wasn't the only one capable of suppression. He had acted in innocence regarding his omission, thinking it incidental all along, once living near to where Kate had also been brought up, because neither of them would ever have known one another as children, as Kate had been born a couple of years after Andrew and his mother had left the district. Yes, he had left it out, certainly, but not for any of the reasons now going through Kate's mind.

After the events that evening it was clear to Andrew that he would be going back to Tottenham the following weekend on his own. By the time Saturday arrived neither he nor Kate were on particularly good speaking terms with one another. The detachment that was now between them, had caused Kate to go round to her brother Giles each night after work, and by the time she had returned to the flat, Andrew was already asleep. This distancing was uncomfortable for them both, but due to what had gone before, it was inevitable.

The terrace houses in Prentice Street had mostly all seen better days. Though a few showed signs of upkeep, by and large they mainly all looked as if they had been left to the elements, to fade and decay. Number fourteen was no exception, not by a long chalk. In fact, it didn't surprise Andrew when he saw its dilapidation, for it fitted in with the picture he had in his mind, that had been conjured up from his visit to the solicitors. Standing now in front of the house he remembered going in and out with his mother, holding her hand firmly for reassurance. He walked awkwardly up to the front door, took his father's door key out of his jacket pocket and placed it in the lock. This one was not going to relent and open so easily like his own, it was stiff and the lock in need of lubrication, so it took a couple of determined turns by Andrew before it was willing to open. He pushed the door forward and peered inside as it swung back slowly on its hinges. The hallway was stark and empty except for an old umbrella stand that held one faded, bat-winged-shaped brolly. Local newspapers and junk mail lay in cascades on the floor and crackled under his feet as he proceeded down the hall. The front room had been used as the main lounge and was still as it was when Andrew and his mother had lived there, for by the look of things nothing had ever been changed. It was not untidy which was a relief to Andrew, but rather precise to the point of annoyance. Small ornaments neatly in place on the mantelpiece, and books tidily placed rigidly in order of size stood irritatingly together. He noted the sideboard and the rusted biscuit tin that Gerald Hillier had informed him about, the one that had held the £79, the only money found in the property. He went out and down the corridor to the kitchen, which was as bare as it was lifeless. Thankfully, the council had done the job of clearing out any remaining remnants of food and taken away the rubbish from the bin. Andrew gazed out of the kitchen window and saw the swing that he had played on as a child, halfway down the garden. It stood there like a testament to another time, now waiting for another child to claim it. He didn't want to be here, going through these rooms. It wasn't exactly painful, the memories, it was that he felt no sense of belonging. Such a good job had been done to eradicate these early years that even the sight of a plaything in the garden couldn't conjure up any sense of emotional response. As he turned away from the window he distinctly heard a sound, footsteps coming into the hall. He stood still, almost rigid by the side of the kitchen table and listened as the steps could be heard coming nearer. Then a voice called out to the empty stillness of the house.

'Andy, are you there?'

It was Kate; she had taken a chance and followed him shortly after he had left. Not knowing if she was doing the right thing or not but on the spur of the moment deciding to do it anyway.

'I'm in the kitchen,' Andrew called out to her, wondering why she had come after him. Maybe she had the curiosity for the house that he decidedly lacked.

Kate came into the room hesitantly.

'I didn't expect to see you here,' said Andrew rather matter of factly.

'Neither did I, until after you left this morning.'

They looked at one another awkwardly. A lingering silence stood between them.

'There's nothing much, as you can see for yourself,' Andrew said stating facts not feelings. No hint of emotion was forthcoming, not here, not in this place.

'Well, we'd better go and take a look upstairs then,' Kate replied with an air of authority.

The top of the house was a replica of the downstairs by way of its neatness and austerity. The room that had been slept in by his parents, then for all those years solely by his father, felt unnatural for Andrew to enter into. A bedroom once occupied by adults and a place expecting to be classed out of bounds even now by a grown-up son. He went in and glanced slowly around at the contents of the room. Nothing particular met his eyes, except for an old, worn suitcase that was slightly sticking out from under the bed. He pulled it out from underneath the metal frame, noting the heavy pull from whatever lay inside. Trying to open it was impossible as it had been locked.

'How are you getting on?' he called out to Kate who was in the next room.

'Fine', she answered from the room next door, the one that Andrew had slept in as a child. Though the truth was she felt an intruder, peering into a room that appeared to have been frozen in time. In front of her propped up by the end of the bed was a faded, yellow teddy bear, and at the back of the room in a corner was a dated collection of boy's toys in a large, worn-out cardboard box. Kate went over and started looking at the playthings that Andrew most certainly would have spent his leisure time with. She started to finger the model toys, turning them over to see what exactly was there. And then she came across some other things in the box, beautifully dressed plastic dolls buried beneath a pile of jigsaws. She started to finger them, turning them over to see exactly what else might be there. As the layer of jumbled dolls moved apart she noticed some other things that were rather unusual for a boy's room, tiny plastic hair slides, and flower-embroidered handkerchiefs still in cellophane wrappings. The strangeness of the find was perplexing. She didn't want to linger and went hurriedly to join Andrew in the front bedroom. He was still trying to fathom out how to get into the case, having failed to find a key that might open the lock.

'Nothing doing', he said as he yet again tried to force the suitcase apart.

'Hang on and I'll get a knife from the kitchen,' Kate told him before disappearing downstairs, eager for Andrew to open the case so that they could both leave the house and its echoes of an uncharitable past. She found the cutlery drawer and took her requirement from a collection of assorted utensils. But as she went to make her way out of the kitchen, she noticed something uncannily familiar hanging up behind the kitchen door, and in a split second was reminded of her own childhood or, to be more precise, one event in particular that was forever imprinted on her mind. Inches away from her was a leather jerkin, with no sleeves, but marked by heavy stains on the tanned leather, with deep pockets in the front and large unmistakable brown buttons. She knew this had to be the one, even before she noted the missing third button. Vivid memories of a day many years ago now faced her, reminding her of when she had lost her bus fare, and a smiling face had offered to carry her home from outside the gates of her junior school. She had said no, but the man had just laughed and picked her up placing her high up on his shoulders, so that the leather from his jerkin had caressed her legs. He kept telling her not to be afraid and that he would take her all the way home, after he had given her some sweets because she was so pretty. Kate felt a chilliness start to come over her as she remembered the man saying that the sweets were in his house and it was not far away. But she also remembered what her mother had told her to do if something like this ever happened, so that she had swiftly started to kick and punch the front of the leather jerkin with all her might, and somehow in her frantic action managed to pull a button off, whilst screaming out loud to draw attention to her terrifying situation. Within seconds she had been roughly put down on the hard pavement and then Kate had run, she had run for all she was worth, leaving the man shouting back after her.

Like Andrew she had closed a chapter on her past, but for a completely different reason. And now it had re-emerged as fresh in her mind as if it had only just happened. She moved past the jerkin and as she did so, the smell, that unforgettable smell of some kind of machine oil, was there even now. It had permeated the leather just as it had done with her mind.

'Kate!' Andrew's voice called out suddenly in earnest. 'Don't come back up here, wait for me down there.'

But she was already numbly making her way out into the hall towards the flight of stairs.

'Just don't come in here, please,' he pleaded unsuccessfully, trying to block her from the front bedroom. She wasn't going to let this go, there was more to this unfolding story and the oddities lying in his old room, let alone the meshing in of her life. She pushed him away forcibly just as she had done with his father and courageously entered the main bedroom. In the middle of the floor was the suitcase, now opened by a small key that Andrew had chanced upon whilst Kate was in the kitchen. Its contents were not hidden any more just like the rapidly evolving past. Magazines, the nature of which were abhorrent, and even from their front covers evident of the repulsive abuse of young children that was waiting inside their vile pages.

Kate turned away with repugnance, glancing momentarily at Andrew who was standing there with his own private disgust. There was nothing for either of them to say. The house had given up its ghastly secrets and had revealed more than it had ever intended. And when in silence they made their way out into the dulling sunlight, there was a yearning for a sharing of grief for each tainted childhood that for so long had lain buried in the past.

Lost Time

'I still can't believe it's really you!'

'Yes, it's me,' said Maureen into the telephone.

'It must be thirty years at least,' said the voice on the other end of the line, sounding full of amazement.

In actual fact it was almost thirty-three years, but Maureen didn't mention it. However many years it was, it had been far too long there was no question about that.

'If it hadn't been for that new Families Found site on the Internet then I don't think that I would have traced you at all,' replied Maureen to her long-lost sister Barbara.

And that was the truth of it. It was by pure luck that Maureen had come across the site. She really didn't think she would have a cat-in-hell's chance of locating any of her remaining family members, let alone her older sister. It was the first site of its kind that she had tried and as it was professionally constructed and with a modest joining fee, she had decided to give it a go. In the 'search family member' as was the term used on the website, Maureen typed the same married name as her sister's had been, Carr, followed by her first name, Barbara, and immediately there were some results. Looking down the list one entry stood out, for under the name Barbara Carr was the name Victoria under children. Maureen remembered that Barbara had been expecting a child when she got married and at the time said to her that, if the baby was a girl, Victoria was the name she was considering giving her. The location didn't ring any bells though, Horsham, but as Maureen's husband Stuart used to change jobs like other people changed their underwear, as their mother Iris used to say, it was feasible.

Because Stuart hadn't been at all liked by Iris, or indeed their father Bernard, the eventual family rift had started long before there was even talk of a wedding. In fact, Stuart's own father thought he wasn't up to much as a son and that he wouldn't do anything with his life except probably waste it. But they were all to be proved wrong, at least with regard to making a financial success was concerned. Early in their marriage Stuart had managed to get his act together, Barbara told Maureen, and found employment with a company in Edgware that manufactured fire doors and both he and Barbara's lives started to change for the better. He became known as 'Fire Door Man' in the trade she said, and so keen was he in the promotion and selling of the various product lines that he rapidly became an Executive Director and, after being awarded shares in the company, the world of flame-retardant fire doors became his oyster. His private life however was quite a different kettle of fish. On the surface he seemed the happy family man with an executive lifestyle and all the trimmings. However frequent business trips abroad had given him ample opportunity to indulge his desire to be unfaithful. And in various five-star hotels in numerous capital cities around the world where everything and everyone has their price, he took full advantage of what was easily offered.

'Dad was right all along not to trust him,' said Barbara as she gave Maureen a synopsis of what had gone wrong with their marriage. 'I didn't want to believe it at first, although I had my suspicions, but it was when I went out to join him when he was on a long business trip to Hong Kong that I found something that had been left behind from the night before.'

'Why didn't you contact any of us?'

'Too ashamed and I couldn't have coped with the 'I told you so's".

Maureen heard her sister sniff the air as she fought to hold back rising emotions. She started to think back, remembering the huge row that had taken place when her sister had announced that she intended to marry Stuart and that she was pregnant. Her mother did attend the wedding along with Maureen, but not Bernard her father; he said after the event that he didn't care if he ever saw hide nor hair of them again, and that is precisely what happened. Iris and Maureen did keep up contact for a while and visited Barbara a few times after the wedding, but due to the upsets at home with Maureen's father each time they returned home, Iris reluctantly stopped going to visit her oldest daughter and any further contact ceased.

Eventually both their parents passed away in quick succession of one another which was often the case. Their mother Iris having right up until just before her death secretly sent a Christmas card each year to Barbara's address, but she never received a card back or heard from her daughter.

'Anyway,' continued Barbara regaining her composure before she took up the story of what had transpired after the Hong Kong trip, 'Although he tried to squirm his way out of things, I wasn't having any of it and, to cut a long story short, once I was back in the UK I started divorce proceedings. Fortunately, it wasn't messy like some people end up going through, and to be honest it was a relief.'

'You mean you weren't upset at the end?' Maureen asked.

'It's hard to be sad for someone that you hardly ever saw. He often worked long hours and liked to drink with the lads, so what with that and the constant travelling away from home, I had got used to my own company. Plus, there was Vicky, of course, without her I think it might have been different. She's been a real credit.'

'You sound very proud,' replied her sister.

Barbara certainly was, for Vicky had turned into a very attractive and focused young woman. She had for a time been a relatively successful catwalk model, and then when her time was up, she decided to run her own business and had used some of her savings to open a dress agency, which specialised in upmarket and designer label fashions.

'I have a lovely life, and don't miss Stuart at all. Vicky lives only ten minutes' drive from me and we have nights out and do lots of things together,' Barbara told her. And then she added, 'But of course I've never forgotten you. How could I, my own sister? I've often felt bitter about the way things turned out and used to blame myself for the cutting of the family ties, and also because we've lost so much time.'

'Is that what prompted you to put your details on the 'Families Found' site?' asked Maureen keenly.

'Firstly, it was more out of curiosity really. Does that sound awful?'

Maureen knew exactly what her sister meant by all this. She too had been hit by the curiosity bug. For some people it took the form of voyeurism, so she was led to believe from what she had read about other similar contact web sites. People would hit various sites, find lost family, friends, workmates etc. and exchange one or two emails and that would be that. Some just found out information, digested it and if it was to their liking i.e. that the old friend hadn't moved on with their lives or done very much, they would smirk inwardly with self-satisfaction and then the contact would cease. But for someone whose curiosity was wrapped up in a compelling desire to connect then the end result was a meeting. For both sisters this was the achievable goal that each of them now had their minds set upon. Eventually during that first call, Maureen and Barbara found the time to make arrangements for a further one the following week to which this time Barbara would be the one to telephone. They started alternating the calls each week and discussed meeting up sometime at the beginning of August. Barbara was shortly going away to Malta with a group from a charity that she helped out with on an ad-hoc basis. She informed Maureen that a spare place had arisen at the last minute and she had taken up the offer. The group were a fun bunch and Barbara was looking forward to the holiday and just as much the return and arranging to meet up with her long-lost sister. Maureen too looked forward to their meeting, the exact date to be agreed between them when Barbara returned from her holiday, and when it was her turn once again to telephone.

But the anticipated call never came.

'Maybe you've got the date wrong and she's coming back next week,' said Phil, Maureen's husband, as he noticed his wife intently studying the calendar one Sunday morning.

'I don't think so. Look I marked it,' Maureen lifted the calendar from its hook behind the kitchen door. A photo of a sleepy, over-fed, ginger-and-white cat stared back at her from the top of the glossy page. 'See, there it is, I never make a mistake. I distinctly remember writing it on after our last phone call.'

'You could always telephone her, it wouldn't do any harm,' he replied taking off his gardening shoes and placing them carefully onto some old newspaper.

'No, I couldn't do that. It's for her to ring me. That's what we agreed. Anyway maybe she has her reasons,' Maureen said putting the calender back on the kitchen door.

'You could be right, maybe something's come up and she's been busy. You know yourself what it's like when you get back from holiday,' said Phil trying to be tactful.

But Maureen didn't think that Barbara's lack of a telephone call was due to her being snowed under with things to do. She thought the answer obvious. There must have been a sudden change of heart by her sister. Barbara had simply decided not to go ahead with the meeting, possibly due to cold feet, and while away in sunnier climes had thought it best not to disturb the status quo and open up any old family sores.

But Barbara hadn't had cold feet, she had suffered a major stroke one morning in her kitchen. She was rushed to hospital but sadly didn't recover.

Vicky, like the dutiful daughter that she was, went ahead and meticulously made all the arrangements for her mother's funeral herself, right down to the very last detail. She included everyone that her mother had known including, of course, the local charity group that Barbara had helped out with which was extremely well represented. However, she did not invite Maureen not because she didn't want her there but because she didn't know that Maureen and her mother had found one another again. Barbara had not said one single word to her daughter about Maureen contacting her, wanting to surprise her when she finally met up with her long-lost sister. She had had it all planned out that on her return from Malta when it was her turn to call, she would invite Maureen over for lunch and Vicky would be there too. Barbara would just say to Vicky that there was going to be a surprise waiting for her. She was really looking forward to meeting her sister again after so many years; it would no doubt be a really long lunch as they both had to make up for so much lost time.

The Goat

They had been travelling along this unfamiliar stretch of road for about three miles now, desperately trying to find their way to the coast road, which was the only one that would successfully lead them back to their hotel. But with the absence of any signposts in this region, and an island map that would challenge the skills of even the most experienced of travellers, they both knew that they were well and truly lost.

'I don't understand it, I was sure that we were going the right way,' said Matt with more than a hint of annoyance in his voice.

Sally didn't say a word, knowing that if she did there would be the possibility of a full scale row breaking out, and that was something that after such a memorable day spent snorkelling in the turquoise waters alongside Speyside, she most certainly didn't want to happen.

The holiday had only just begun for her and Matt, it being their first time somewhere so faraway and in a location so gloriously exotic as this one.

'What about Tobago?' she had said one chilly Saturday in mid-September. 'There are some great deals to be had, and we could go away before our gloomy winter sets in.'

Matt looked up briefly from the new book that he was absorbed in reading. It was called 'How to Manage Your Work More Efficiently.' He had literally dozens of books in this vein around the house, each of them having been read and digested, but to all intents and purposes there never seemed to be much change in the way Matt approached his demanding job. Although he didn't realize it, he was like someone trying to understand why they always made the same mistakes in their wrong choice of partner, pouring over self-help books in the delusion that the next chapter would possess the hidden key that would unlock them from their misery. Except Matt wasn't looking for any quick fixes, he was searching for more than that in the business hardbacks that he almost constantly devoured. Or so he kept telling himself.

'Wouldn't we have to have loads of injections, and anyway what's so special about Tobago, it's not one of those far-off places that instantly springs to mind.' Matt replied before going back to his reading.

Sally came over to the sofa and sat down beside him.

'To answer your first question, yes, we would need some jabs a few weeks before travel I've checked it out at the doctors, and secondly take a look at this.' She handed him a colour brochure. 'This is the reason why it's so special.'

Matt put down his book and took the holiday brochure from Sally.

'Wow, it certainly looks great,' he said looking at the glossy pictures of palm-fringed beaches with sand the colour of soft brown sugar and beckoning blue water. The information in the brochure said that development was apparently kept to an acceptable limit; no rows and rows of hotels packed together along a strip like some of the other tropical island destinations. It stated that the beauty of Tobago and its wildlife had been preserved, and that was the basis of its distinctiveness. He started to study the pages of various beachside hotels, and after a few minutes handed the brochure back to his wife.

'If it's this good, it certainly will be a holiday to remember,' Matt added, to which Sally knew meant they were as good as being on their way.

Now on this unknown road in the middle of nowhere, with the last rays of daylight starting to fade, Matt was thinking that getting lost on their second day on the island was the last thing he wanted to remember his holiday for. Due to his increasing frustration, his overall driving became somewhat erratic, and he started to take unexpected corners rather sharply, with the inevitable result that the car started to skid as it went into a winding bend.

'Matt!' Sally could contain herself no longer and shouted out to him, 'For goodness sake, take it easy!'

But Matt wasn't listening, he continued with his hazardous driving until Sally suddenly let out an ear-splitting scream as a large, dark shape was seen through the windscreen heading directly towards them. By the time Matt had applied the brakes of the hire car, they had already heard and felt an almighty bang. The car and both its occupants shook violently at the impact which was so unexpected and instantaneous, and delivered such a force, it was as if they had just been thrown into the side of a house. Abruptly the car came to a halt.

'We've hit something,' said Sally trembling all over with shock.

'Well, I would think that's bloody obvious,' Matt replied rubbing the back of his neck. 'And to crown it all, I think I've got whiplash.'

Sally ignored her husband's moaning and opened the passenger door and got out of the car to get some air. She could see the front was damaged with a large dent in the bumper and part of the bonnet also. She called over to her husband to tell him.

'What about the tyres?' called out Matt from his open window. Sally walked round the vehicle checking.

'No, seems they're all OK,' she replied, still shaken from what had just happened.

Matt tried the engine which started straight away. 'OK, Sal get back in and we can get going', he told her.

But Sally didn't want to get in, she wanted to see what exactly had been on the receiving end of the car's bumper.

'Hey Sal, where do you think you are going?' Matt shouted out to her as she started to move away from the car. Ignoring her husband, she looked around and immediately stopped short when she saw what was not that far away from her, and covered her mouth with her hands in disbelief. There lying by the left-hand side of the road was the body of a goat. It had partially ended up on the start of a small, grassy verge where it had landed after being tossed in the air by the collision. The back legs were both sticking bolt upright along with the rear portion directly on the road itself with the rest of the poor creature stretched out on the grass with its front legs pointing in the direction of some rather tall trees. From the expression on its face it looked as if it was in a deep slumber which more than indicated to Sally that it was well and truly dead.

'At least it didn't suffer,' announced Matt when he eventually managed to come over to join her and assess the situation.

'What are we going to do about it?' said Sally showing concern.

'What do you mean, there's nothing we can do, we'll just have to leave it here,' Matt replied with irritation at the appalling scenario.

Sally turned around to face her husband.

'But you killed it, Matt, and all because you wouldn't listen to me and slow down,' she looked harshly at him stating the fact of the matter.

But as usual he didn't want to admit that he had done something wrong and skirted around the issue.

'Oh, come on, we most probably would have knocked it for six anyway, stupid thing was already wandering about in the road.'

'So that makes it OK to go and drive off to God knows where, as if you haven't already forgotten we're lost,' said Sally who was starting to lose her patience.

'So, what do you want me to do about it?'

Matt's face had taken on a surly appearance. All he wished for right now was to be back at the hotel crashing out on their comfortable, queen-size bed with a rum cocktail in his hand.

'For a start you can get hold of the head and I'll take the feet, and we'll move it across to the side, we can't leave it lying half on half off of the road.' Sally went towards the stiff animal.

'Come on hurry up before another vehicle appears or we'll too be in the same horizontal position,' she picked up the two hind legs.

'I can't do it, Sal,' Matt said starting to bottle out.

'Oh, for goodness sake, Matt, grab its ears and drag it over, it won't take a minute.'

But the goat was heavier than either of them thought it would be. It was rather a big beast, nothing at all like the ones back home in England, with this particular variety almost resembling a pint-size Shetland pony. Eventually after a few attempts they had managed to get the animal completely over to the verge by the side of road.

'Well that's all done with, come on, let's get going,' Matt turned away and started to walk back to the hire car.

'I'll be with you in a minute,' Sally called out to him giving the goat one last, final check over.

Then just before she turned to go, she heard some movement from behind a tree near where the goat was positioned. Thinking it was more than likely another member of the herd, and not wishing for any more unexpected animal encounters, she started to slip carefully away. But then a deep voice that seemed to come out of nowhere called out to her.

'An' another one bites the dust!'

Immediately Sally stopped in her tracks realizing that someone was watching her. Turning cautiously around, she started to stare very closely through the gaps in between the various tree trunks, until her eyes spotted the figure of a rather tall Rastafarian. His substantial head was outlined by thick dreadlocks, proudly displayed like the plumage of a bird of paradise, skimming his shoulders and hanging right down his back. From the way he was sitting it looked as if he had been comfortably seated for a long time, possibly most of the afternoon, and in an ideal position that would have easily enabled him to be able to see the unpleasant event that had only just taken place. He got up slowly from where he was sitting and sauntered over to approach her.

'If it was yours I'm truly sorry about what happened,' she blurted out.

The Rastafarian looked intensely at Sally, making her feel uneasy as if his eyes were searching out her soul.

'Oh yeah, I believe you do. But it's de man over there dat has de problem,' he said nodding in the direction of Matt and the hire car.

The Rastafarian's astuteness struck a chord with Sally.

The noise of Matt impatiently sounding the car's horn further emphasised his point.

'I think he hasn't quite got the hang of 'chillin out' just yet,' she replied with embarrassment for her husband's poor attitude.

'Hmm,' the Rasta said and stroked his blotchy grey beard.

'Look, about the goat, can we give you some money for it?' Sally asked.

He shook his head and its mane of cascading dreadlocks.

'Tain't mine, it belong to 'im up there now,' he answered raising his eyes to the sky.

But the person whom it did belong to?' Sally said, keen to get the matter sorted out.

'Oh, I knows 'im alright, hmm.'

'Can you tell him, that we truly didn't mean it to happen, and we'll be happy to compensate him for the loss of his animal. He can contact us at…'

'The Swaying Palm Trees 'otel,' the Rastafarian said cutting in finishing Sally's sentence for her.

'How on earth did you know that?'

He gave her a huge grin and pointed to the number plate on the car.

'Dere's a small palm tree top of the plate, so everyone can tell where you're staying.'

Again, the horn was sounded.

Sally raised her arm indicating that this time she was coming, and rounded off the conversation with the

Rastafarian, but not before obtaining the right directions back to the hotel and exchanging names.

'Oh an' by the way, girl,' he said just as she made a move to go, 'Dere's something you got wrong.'

Sally looked rather puzzled.

'It's called limmin, what we do 'ere. It's our way o' saying 'chillin out'. Nice an' easy does it.'

'I'll remember to tell my husband,' she replied, catching the grinning gaze of the Rasta's eyes.

What on earth have you been saying to that guy?' said Matt when Sally got back into the car.

'I've been trying to sort this mess out.'

'Well I bet you've gone and made things a damn sight worse.'

'Oh, just shut it, Matt,' Sally said firmly, 'I've got the directions how to get back so just pipe down.'

Surprisingly, he obeyed, his keenness to get going overriding any desire to argue. He started the engine and proceeded to drive off in a much more cautious manner than he had previously done before the accident. Now armed with a straightforward set of directions that Sally through her chance meeting had been fortunate to obtain, they found their way easily back to the welcome street lights of the main town road, and in no time at all were back at the Swaying Palm Trees Hotel.

Matt very quickly forgot about the fate of the poor goat, but not about the pain in his neck and the throbbing headache that had developed shortly after they had returned. The hotel's on-call doctor promptly came and checked him out, and Matt was told that he was very lucky in that he only had a mild form of whiplash, and the advice was for him not to overdo things, to rest up and stay out of the sun for a while. He did manage to fill out an accident report and give his version of what had happened to the local police, and hire car company, which was taxing enough for him, and afterwards he retreated to the bedroom where he stayed for almost two days.

In some ways, Sally was relieved to find that she now had some time and space between herself and her husband. She knew that Matt's behaviour could be 'difficult' at the best of times, but his appalling attitude towards not only her, but to the unfortunate goat, was starting to show him in a slightly different light to the one she was familiar with in the past, and frankly she didn't like what she saw emerging.

Now due to Matt's incapacitation, Sally had free reign to go and do whatever she pleased, for a short while at any rate. Initially, after the events of the previous day, she stayed at the hotel complex content with swimming in the gentle warm waters of the crystal lagoon that edged the hotel's private beach. A welcome change from yesterday's fiasco she thought to herself.

By the following day, both Matt and Sally had discarded any thoughts about the accident, thinking that as it had been reported, that was the end to the matter. Nothing however could have been further from the truth. For although the police and the hire company were satisfied with the story of the events on that day, there was someone else who had not forgotten so easily.

Shortly after breakfast that morning, there was a telephone call for Sally. Although Matt still had the remains of his headache, he was other than that and a stiff neck, relatively fine. He noted his wife's recognising response as she listened to the caller, speaking only briefly before replacing the receiver.

'What was that all about?' he asked itching to know who might be calling for her.

'Hm, oh someone for me,' she moved over to pick up her bag and started checking a few of the things inside.

'Are you planning to go out somewhere?' he asked.

'Yes, Hamilton says there will a car ready to pick me up in about half an hour'.

'Who on earth's Hamilton?'

‘The chap I meet the other day, you remember when we had that unfortunate accident,’ she said checking her appearance in the mirror above the dressing table.

‘You mean that guy with the dreadlocks?’ Matt said in amazement, moving himself up from his position on the bed.

‘Yes, that very nice Rastafarian. Don’t worry Matt, I’m a big girl now, I can look after myself’.

She picked up her bag and moved towards the door.

‘And if you don’t mind me asking, just where are you going?’ Matt asked his wife.

Sally turned briefly to look back at her husband.

‘I’m going to see a man about a goat.’

And quick as a flash she was gone, leaving Matt’s curiosity to ponder over just where his wife was off to, and what might transpire from the outcome. His heart sank with worry that the episode of the unfortunate creature was not dispensed with. Not by a long chalk was it over he realised, not in the slightest.

Still suffering with the remnants of his headache, he took some paracetamols and tried to get some more rest. But instead of a welcome sleep, the type that washes over and soothes, he was plagued by images of bearded goats, possessing chattering teeth all herding straight towards him. He tried to wake up, but was pulled back down into his slumber again, so that the nightmare continued. It was as if he was riding a horse that had to complete a torturous race, and all he could do was to hold on tight until it had come to the finish.

The relief Matt felt when he did eventually wake up out of his nightmare was overwhelming. His blinding headache had left him, so that he could hardly get up quick enough and get himself dressed. Firstly, he went off out for a walk in the hotel’s gardens, before returning to sit on the balcony. That was where Sally found him when she returned a few hours later. Unusually for Matt he was deep in thought, just staring out to the ocean, which formed part of their view. He looked utterly forlorn, lost even, so that as she went up to speak to him, she placed a hand tenderly on his shoulder.

'Did you see a man about a goat?' he enquired; his gaze still directed out across the horizon.

'Yes, I saw him, and he wants to see you too.'

Matt turned towards her, his eyes starting to moisten.

'Oh, Matt, it's not as bad as all that,' Sally said starting to stroke his hair, wiping stray, wispy strands from his forehead.

'Then why does he want to see me?'

'I think he wants to give you a little lesson in 'Limmin.'

The following day, at around 1 o'clock, the same car that had initially been sent for Sally, returned to pick both of them up and drove them away from the shoreline up high into the interior, away from the island's main road through a route that took them into a thick tropical landscape, before panning out on a plateau of luscious, green countryside. Like a lot of the vehicles used by the locals it was old but very tough and sturdy, and sported a remarkable interior of tan-coloured, real leather seats. Cracked and worn they may have been, but there was still a bit of life left in them yet. Naturally, Sally and Matt were retracing their steps, and before long the spot where the accident had taken place came into view. The goat itself had not been spoken of after the initial conversation the day beforehand, directly after Sally had returned to the hotel. For Matt this had been a welcome respite, and although he was relieved to hear Sally's assurances, he still couldn't fathom out what was in store for him and was more than apprehensive.

'Dat's where they found 'im,' said Lewis the driver of the car, pointing over to the verge at the side of the road. As if Matt needed anymore reminding.

'Nasty business alright, ain't it,' he glanced up in his mirror to catch Matt's eye.

'Dem goats, never knows where dey gonna spring from,' he added.

Just beyond the scene of the accident, Lewis turned off the road and drove along a narrow, dirt track that had an assortment of candy-coloured houses and small, tin shacks dotted along its side. Children and dogs were scattered along the route and waved and giggled with embarrassment into their hands as they caught Sally smiling back at them. Lewis started to slow the car down, before stopping on a corner outside one of the shacks. It appeared that a celebration of sorts was taking place out the back in the garden, with lots of people going in, but very few if any coming out. And all around the air was filled with the aroma of spicy cooking that smelt like a delicious curry.

'There's Hamilton,' said Sally as Lewis led then through, indicating towards one of the tables, which housed a huge ornamented glass bowl full of a fascinating concoction that included fresh fruit juices. She seemed totally at ease with everything that was going on around her, which puzzled Matt no end, because he himself didn't have a clue as to what it was all about.

'Come on over an' join the party!' Hamilton called, holding up a glass of the intriguing mixture.

'So, this is the man 'imself,' he said leaning back against the table, sizing Matt up as he rather reluctantly came over.

'Here 'ave yourself a drink.'

Matt took the glass of bright juice from Hamilton's powerful hand and took a swig. Immediately he felt the sudden impact from its contents as it slid down the back of his throat and started to cough.

'Phew, that's got quite a kick,' he said shaking his head as the drink started to flow through him, 'what on earth's in it?'

'You'll have to ask de gentleman who made it, the party host, Mr Williams.'

Hamilton nodded to a small, elderly man who was standing right next to him.

'Mr Williams 'ere has been wanting to talk to you about Lazarus.'

The old man looked keenly at Matt, his opaque eyes focusing hard at the young man standing in front of him.

'Lazarus was my goat,' he said softly.

'And I think if you'll excuse us, me an' Matt here got some talking to do,' he said looking directly at the young man.

Sally and Hamilton complied and moved away. The old man continued looking intensely into Matt's face for a while before he continued speaking.

'I suppose you think I want to punish you in some way for what you done to Lazarus. Give you a scolding or telling off, eh? Something like dat going through your mind?'

Matt was completely taken aback with the old man's accuracy, unnerving him, as if he had access to his thoughts.

'And where would dat get us? You knows you done wrong, I knows it too, and Lazarus, well,' he paused for a second in reflection, 'to tell the truth he was a lot o' trouble dat old Billy goat, I can tell you. Reminded me of my youngest son,' he added with a hint of reminiscence.

'But don't think that made it alright for you to drive like the wind without a care for no one and nothing,' he added firmly shaking a thin, half-curled finger at Matt.

Matt looked away shamefully.

'Come and get some food, boy, you looks like you need it.'

The old man put his arm round the younger in a fatherly manner, and then proceeded to take him over to a much larger table, which had a huge receptacle full of a rich-looking curry in its centre. Steaming fluffy, white rice was sitting in another pot, and home-made chutneys and lime pickles were alongside for the taking. Mr Williams served Matt up a large portion.

'This is really tasty,' said Matt as he started to tuck into his food, 'it's one of the best curries I've had for a long time'.

'Old Lazarus, 'e weren't much good when he was alive, but 'im sure making up for it now,' said Mr Williams starting to laugh.

'Oh, my God, you don't surely mean that…' Matt answered, abruptly putting down his fork.

'Yes, goat curry, very good for you. My wife Adelaide, she 'as made a special recipe. It's quite a while since we 'ad goat, that's why we is all here today,' he said indicating to the crowd of people.

'But I don't understand, how could you possibly bear to eat him?' Matt said before placing his plate down on the table.

'Why not? Oh yes, he had a name an' all, but you sees Lazarus was very lazy and unruly. He wouldn't do 'as he was told. He just used to go off on his own and get 'imself into all sorts of trouble, fightin' an' all. The other goats didn't care for him either, so all in all he caused a lot of problems in the neighbourhood,' Mr Williams replied.

'Is that what happened when I knocked him over? Had he gone off then?'

'Oh yes, been gone missing again that day. I used to tie 'im up on a long piece of rope, but was no good, if he wanted 'e could bite right through, he had a good set of teeth on him, and then, he was away.'

'And if I hadn't driven so fast, he wouldn't now be the main ingredient of this curry,' said Matt morosely looking over at the food table.

Mr William's looked into Matt's eyes, and for the first time he saw the young man's true sense of remorse.

'Well, I can see that you are now sorry for what 'as happened, so we will say no more. Anyway, I thought you were enjoying your food,' said the old man going over to retrieve Matt's plate. 'Everyone here says the best thing about Lazarus is that 'e has made the finest curry they have eaten in years,' Mr Williams added so that Matt could hopefully resume his meal without feeling guilty.

Before long, the rest of that extraordinary day gradually blended into evening, and the air that had been full of delicious cooking transcended into one full of the rhythm of haunting music from the village's steel band. Hamilton was their leader, and also sung some of his own compositions with deep, meaningful lyrics that came out of a life spent in thoughtful contemplation of the ways of many.

The lights of flickering candles around the garden gave it a reverent feel, and towards the end of the evening when Mr Williams spoke to thank everyone for coming, he added a few words of prayer that included Lazarus, thanking him for giving them such a fine meal on such a memorable day as this one.

For Matt the day that had started so ominously had turned out to be one so unimaginable from the one he had initially pictured in his mind, so that when it was time to leave he didn't want to go, thinking that if he did then the incredible warm feeling and contentment he now felt inside would not stay with him, that it would swiftly evaporate. He looked sadly at the faces of the many people he had met, watching them still enjoying themselves in the last remnants of the evening.

'Well, I think you finally got the hang of it now,' said Hamilton as he sauntered over to say goodbye.

'I'm not with you, H,' said a rather intoxicated Matt.

'Yes, you are, but you don't know it, Matt,' said Sally whispering into her husband's ear.

'Limmin man, you *finally* got the flow,' said Hamilton beaming.

'But how do I hold on to it?'

'You'll 'ave to find your own way,' said the dignified Rastafarian. 'Now you 'ave it it's up to you not to lose it.'

And as Matt and Sally reluctantly walked towards Lewis and his waiting car, Matt knew full well that it wasn't the only thing that he wanted to retain.

Lilac Time

Sylvia Marshall was the sort of woman who always got what she wanted in life. Consequently, she had led a very easy existence because of this demand which was usually, if not always, made upon her long suffering yet thoroughly devoted husband Roger. So that when Sylvia announced to Roger that she had decided that she wanted to move out of their rather charming flat to a house with a garden, he had no alternative in the matter but to comply with her wishes. Such is the downside of total dedication in a marriage. Roger for his part hoped that it would be a fanciful whim of his wife's and that once she realised the effort involved, not to mention the cost, she would soon drop the subject. Unfortunately, that was not to be the case. For Sylvia threw herself furiously into the whole escapade, as she saw it, of looking for suitable properties within a five-mile radius from where they were living.

'Well at least she hasn't set her sights on another area,' said Lionel, Roger's long- standing friend as they walked out onto the eighteen-hole course of their local golf club. 'Think yourself lucky for small mercies.'

'It just seems such an upheaval at our time of life, I mean I've not that long retired and the flat had always seemed fine,' replied Roger, pulling his bag of clubs quickly along behind him, keen to get to the first hole.

'What was that you said about a garden?'

'Oh yes, that's the long and short of it. Sylvia has her heart set on one.'

'Yet you've lived without greenery ever since you've been married,' said Lionel, getting a coin out of his trouser pocket ready for tossing to see who would tee off first. 'Does Sylvia know much about gardening?' he added.

'Not to my knowledge, can't tell a peony from a begonia. But then neither can I so we'll make a fine pair,' answered Roger, smiling unfalteringly across at his friend.

'Well, maybe she'll change her mind when she realises just how much hard work having one entails. Take it from me, lovely as my small patch is, it's still a hard slog to keep it that way.'

But Sylvia had no intention of doing any of the 'hard stuff' herself, no, once they had moved into the house with the garden that was to fulfil her fancy, she had her sights set on employing a gardener to do all the tedious and labour-intensive work. She would only venture into it to admire and occasionally cut selected flowers for bringing into the house. The gardener would be expected to come and keep an eye on things sometime during the week – odd mornings that sort of thing. Yes, she thought to herself that would do very nicely, very nicely indeed.

So, after five weeks of selective searching, the garden was found. The house seemed to be more of an incidental in some bizarre way, for it was the garden that was the main interest having totally won Sylvia over from the moment she had clapped eyes on it through the polished glass of the French windows. And what a garden it was, with large, flowing borders of high-reaching hollyhocks, fabulous fuchsias, and assorted climbing honeysuckle, plus a wide-flowing lawn that ended somewhere almost beyond vision. Or so it appeared to Roger. He was astonished at the sheer scale of it, never for once imagining that there were any properties in the area with anything of that size. The house itself was very ordinary, a standard thirties semi, really nothing to write home about. But looks being deceiving, its best feature by far was hidden away from view behind a pair of gold drapes, that once pulled and tied in swags showed the jewel in its crown to perfection.

Within a short time the deal was sealed. Roger and Sylvia's top floor flat sold almost immediately it went on the market, being in a very desirable residential block with designated parking space, entry phone and not ten minutes' walk away from the best commuter rail link to Waterloo in the vicinity. Silently Roger let his wife take charge of the move, and although he himself was not in the least bit keen on the upheaval, he never once let on. For his pleasure came about seeing her happiness, however much the cost to himself. Watching Sylvia in her excitement, her planning and enthusiasm for the task ahead. That was enough of a reward for Roger. And even if, as in this case, it meant a tremendous effort and a considerable amount of readjustment, being the most major 'want' that his wife had ever expected of him, Roger was not going to refuse.

Because the house was naturally much larger than the flat, all their furniture and modest possessions which had seemed to suit their surroundings so perfectly in their previous home, now appeared completely dwarfed by the size of each of the rooms. As Roger stood looking out through the French windows onto the garden that first morning after they had moved in, it was as if it was only the garden and its many plants and shrubs that was an exact fit. Nothing there seemed to shy away in a corner, getting lost from view. Everything had a place and was featured so that to the naked eye it stood out proudly, almost teasingly, saying to the house, 'Look at me! I'm what people are here for, not you!'

'Isn't it glorious,' said Sylvia coming forward into the room and leisurely walking towards the windows and her husband.

'Yes, it certainly is,' replied Roger.

'Oh, by the way I've found the name of a 'little man', to come and do some work out there,' Sylvia told him.

'Does it need any work doing to it?' said Roger, wondering what now Sylvia had in mind, and above all the cost.

'Roger, it takes a lot of time and effort to achieve something as divine as our beautiful little oasis,' replied his wife. 'Take me for instance, without my weekly visits to Janine for a facial, and my manicures, let alone my regular highlights,' Sylvia paused for a second, 'Well, I think you know what I mean,' she added.

Roger knew exactly what his wife was implying. She was what most people would call 'high maintenance' especially in the beauty department. But it had to be handed to her, Sylvia certainly looked good from all the effort and money spent on maintaining her appearance. Roger, not to mention various members of the golf club, knew that his wife was still a very attractive woman. She had the knack of buying the right clothes for her petite and very trim figure, well-cut suits and toning silk blouses for formal wear, and colour co-ordinated casuals for day to day, plus the devotion to a quality range of expensive make-up and regular appointments at the hairdressers all gave Sylvia a well-turned-out and effortless look. Skill and years of expertise in application was the key to achieving such a flawless and faultless image. Like the garden displayed before them, it all had to have continuous upkeep.

Mr Bradley, the estate agent, had said that the previous owners had employed a chap by the name of Trevor Long who apparently was highly regarded in the area. Having found out his name Sylvia set about tracking the man down. But Trevor Long was a gardener of the old school, no mobile phones or elaborate web sites were necessary for him to obtain work; he had no need for such things as his reputation by word of mouth assured him of enough work to keep most of his local competitors ever envious. He didn't even have a telephone himself, his word being his bond so that when agreed to arrive at a certain day and time he could always be guaranteed to be where intended, and usually a good bit earlier than arranged. A man of very few words, his communication in life came from his skill with his hands that gave such pleasing visual results. Keen to find him, Sylvia asked the local shopkeepers but although one or two of them knew of the gardener, none of them had any idea where he came from. So, after a few more futile attempts, Sylvia decided that the best course of action was to have a look around the neighbourhood. Surely, he must be working somewhere in the locality she thought as she started to walk around the avenues near to her recently acquired home. The houses were all very similar in design and many of them had well-tended front gardens, but mostly the owners were doing them themselves. Sylvia knew that the elusive gardener was out there working somewhere, it was just a case of finding him.

‘Roger, will you get the door!’ Sylvia called out the following morning when she heard the bell and was emptying the dishwasher. Possibly Lionel had decided to pay them a call or rather have a nose round at the new house.

‘You have a visitor,’ said Roger when his wife entered the lounge a few minutes later. ‘This is Mr Long, the gardener. He says you wanted to see him.’

‘Yes, I do,’ said Sylvia, completely taken aback but relieved all the same to see him standing there.

‘I’ve been trying to locate you for the last week. How on earth…’ Sylvia looked the man up and down noticing his shabby clothes, clean but worn, standing in the centre of her new carpet, ‘Oh well, it doesn’t matter you’re here now.’

Trevor didn’t answer but smiled uncomfortably. He was not at ease in customer’s houses, it was outside in their gardens where he was more secure and felt that he belonged.

‘I can start next Monday,’ he told Sylvia, ‘if that’s alright.’ He looked over at Roger seeking his approval.

‘It’s not down to me, it’s my wife who is dealing with the garden,’ Roger said, not wanting to get involved.

‘What time can you come?’ Sylvia asked assuming her authority.

‘8 o’clock.’

‘Regarding the hours and payment,’ Sylvia said keen to get down to business.

Roger’s heart sunk. This was what he had been dreading.

‘It won’t cost much, it’ll be what I always charge,’ said Trevor.

'And exactly how much is that?' Sylvia enquired.

Trevor took out a small pad and pencil from his jacket pocket and started to write some figures down, before handing it over.

'Well, that seems very favourable for the hours and your rates,' she told him, moving the pad over towards Roger so that he could also read it.

'So, I'll see you next Monday then, Mr Long,' Sylvia said ushering him out towards the front door.

'Trevor.'

'OK, Trevor. By the way is there anything you need before then?' Sylvia enquired.

The gardener shook his head.

'Just leave the side open please, then I can come and go like I'm used to.'

And with that he was gone.

'I can't believe it, it seems ridiculously cheap what he's charging,' said Roger as Sylvia returned to the lounge.

'He obviously doesn't think so. Anyway, let's not worry about that, by the sound of things we're going to do very well out of the arrangement I'm sure,' Sylvia said smugly.

Sylvia spoke no truer words that day. For, as the weeks progressed, Trevor Long gave the Marshalls exceptionally good value for their money. More than they could possibly have imagined. In fact, along with the man's total reliability, there was a caring and nurturing that boarded on devotion, as if everything he was touching and planting out there in the earth was in some strange way his own. Roger, who although having no knowledge himself about the skill involved with gardening, couldn't help but notice the dedication that Trevor tirelessly put in, as he occasionally watched discretely from the corner of the French windows.

'Come and smell the beautiful lilacs,' Sylvia called out to Roger one Sunday late in the afternoon. Roger placed his book down and got up from where he had been sitting under the shaded patio and went to find his wife who was somewhere towards the back of the shrubbery. He walked along the sculpted borders that Trevor had spent so much time over, and down the path edged by Victorian rope edging that led to where Sylvia was waiting beside a huge specimen that reached outwards and upwards as if trying to touch the sky above them.

'It's a marvellous bush isn't it. Just smell these wonderful lilacs,' said Sylvia pulling a bough over to meet with Roger's nostrils.

'Phew, that's very heady. I hope you're not thinking of bringing any into the house,' he told her.

'But we always had lilacs in vases in the house when I was a child,' said Sylvia in protest. 'Anyway, the front room needs an additional something in the window.' And with that she started to cut away at the branches with her secateurs. Roger conceded defeat and let her get on with the task she had her mind set upon and returned to the patio and his book.

All things considered, the move had been a surprising success, for not only had it pleased Sylvia having the garden but Roger himself had found it extremely relaxing and enjoyable to sit outside in the warm weather and admire the eye-catching displays that Trevor had cleverly crafted. Yes, he thought to himself, the complete change in lifestyle even at this time in their lives had definitely been worthwhile.

Eventually the year came to a close and, with the turning of the calendar, January came in with a cold wind from the North that left the garden blanketed by a thick layer of snow. Trevor's bulbs that he had previously planted lay snug and warm below the impacted soil, patiently waiting for the easing of frosts and softening of ground, when they would then force their way up to the surface to feel the warming of early morning sunlight that came with clear Spring days. By the middle of March Trevor was again busy out in the Marshalls' garden, with the start of preparations for the coming months in hand and his imagination flowing with ideas for colour planting for the rest of the year. He had an informal consultation with Sylvia but she didn't have any resistance to what he had in mind, being more interested in the results not with any propagation, eager to fill the house with jugs and vases of home-grown flowers. So, as with the previous owners, Trevor had free reign of his domain.

One late morning after Trevor had gone, Sylvia returned from her shopping and stepped out onto the patio. She felt the gentle warmth of the keen sunlight on her face as it penetrated through her carefully powdered complexion. Looking around she noted that much activity was being done to the borders with a lot of clearing having taken place ready for next month's planting. And then suddenly in disbelief Sylvia noted that something was missing from the back of the shrubbery. It was her precious lilac bush; it was no longer visible having been pruned right back by Trevor to within a few inches of the ground. Where it had once grown tall and proud giving the garden complete privacy, now the houses in the avenue back behind the bottom of the fence were in full view. Sylvia rushed down into the garden and up to the place where her beloved bush had previously stood and stared down at the remains.

'Oh no, oh no!' she cried out repeating the words over and over again even after Roger, who had rushed to see what was wrong, helped her back into the house. Wisely he had drawn the curtains to stop her from seeing the obnoxious-looking child who was laughing and staring from the top window of the house that was now in full view from every part of the garden and the French windows. The rest of the day and evening was something of a nightmare for Roger. Eventually he managed to calm Sylvia down. But once her sobbing had ceased, Sylvia's inconsolable desolation started to take on a much different tone. A bottomless pit of rage started to emerge, replacing it with near vitriolic hatred for Trevor Long. Roger could hardly believe his eyes as he watched and listened to his wife plan and scheme how she was going to get her own back on the man for ruining her precious lilac bush. He observed his wife's ranting on and on about how she would ruin him, how she would make sure he would never get any work again. He had seen Sylvia get annoyed on occasion during their long marriage, usually over extremely poor-quality food and bad service in a restaurant, but this was something completely different and worrying in terms of how vindictive she was becoming. When she had finally exhausted herself, miraculously she announced that she was retiring to bed. Roger waited for a good while before deciding to take her up a cup of cocoa and, when he carefully leant over to place it by her bedside cabinet, he noticed with relief that she was already fast asleep.

It came as no surprise to Roger that the following morning he was expected to be the one to inform Trevor Long that his services were no longer required. Sylvia had no intention of speaking to him directly she preferred the slyer tack, using a form of poisoned Chinese whispers to spread as much damage as possible. Roger reluctantly approached Trevor the minute he arrived, waiting for him behind the side gate out of view of Sylvia's gloating gaze. He didn't relish telling him the reason and Trevor could sense that Roger was uneasy with his words especially of the dismissal. For a moment it looked as if he wasn't going to say anything in his defence as if, by way of his silence, Trevor was admitting to his guilt.

'Your wife is no gardener,' he said at last, as one man to another.

'No, that's true, but I think she knows what a lilac bush looks like,' said Roger rising to Sylvia's defence.

'Looks can be misleading,' Trevor replied before adding, 'for it was no lilac, it was a buddleia.'

'Whatever it was, you pruned it so hard that we're totally overlooked now. See,' said Roger pointing towards the back of the lawn and going quite red in the face with the sheer annoyance of the matter.

Trevor looked down the length of the garden to where the bush had once been, glancing at the empty space behind which exposed the dominant backs of the two houses. He stood there motionless for a moment, staring out not at what Sylvia referred to as 'the eyesore', but at the very garden itself, the enchanting haven that he had created over the years.

Sadly, he made for the side gate for the last time but before going through it he had a few final words to say to Roger.

'It will return, just like the butterflies,' he said, and with that he was gone, pulling the gate closed behind him, leaving Roger to wonder just who was in the wrong.

Within days of Trevor's dismissal, Sylvia had already sown her destructive seeds to bring about his downfall. She was like a foot soldier on a misguided mission, speaking to everyone she encountered and almost resorting to writing anonymous letters to the Avenues before Roger found out and for once put his foot down. There didn't seem to be an end to the matter it was as if his wife had taken her anger and turned it into an all-encompassing obsession that filled her every waking thought. Because of this fixation, Roger started to spend more time at his golf club, though generally not on the golf links themselves. Although never before being known as one of the regulars in the bar, very soon he was as familiar as the gleaming row of optics that Jack the barman steadily reached up to when filling Roger's depleted whisky glass.

'You're getting to be part of the fixtures and fittings!' Lionel remarked coming in after a quick round one Sunday with his son David.

Roger ignored his friend's teasing remark and downed the last dregs of his most recent drop of malt.

'Can I get you another?' said Lionel noticing the empty glass.

Roger handed over his glass ready for a refill.

'David not coming in?' Roger asked when Lionel returned with their drinks.

'No, got to get back, Jane's baby's due at any time and he doesn't want to leave her for too long, you know how it is.'

Roger smiled and put the glass to his lips almost downing the whole lot in one go. He tried to imagine what it was like for Lionel's son, the anticipation and excitement of a new arrival to his family. Although he himself wouldn't have minded having children, early on in their marriage Sylvia had had a spell of what was referred to as 'women's troubles', which rather put a damper on the subject. She herself didn't appear to mind, admitting to Lionel's wife Rosemary that in actual fact she had never been in the least bit keen.

'It's that blessed gardener business isn't it?' said Lionel, looking over at Roger, who nodded, knowing full well his face showed that it was still getting him down.

'Can't understand the man, lilac bush you say it was he chopped down?'

'Yes, according to Sylvia. But he was adamant that it was something else, a buddleia whatever that is,' Roger replied knocking back the rest of his whisky.

'The butterfly bush. Well, there is a similarity, but from what Rosemary tells me Sylvia categorically knows her lilac,' Lionel said, before he continued drinking his gin and tonic.

'What was that you just called it,' Roger answered.

'Hmm, oh the butterfly bush, it's the common name for a buddleia. They're attracted to them especially in the summer. Didn't you know? Oh, I forgot you haven't long had a garden,' said Lionel finishing his drink. 'Well I had better be getting a move on, Rosemary's got a nice leg of lamb in the oven. Fancy a round in the week Roger, it's a while since we played?'

'Let me think about it and I'll give you a call.'

When Lionel left the bar, Roger contemplated what had just been said, or what he had just been reminded of, Trevor Long's significant words about the returning butterflies. He retrieved his jacket from the coat stand in the corner of the bar and left the clubhouse. As he made his way home, he had the feeling that both he and Sylvia through their blind ignorance of the ways of nature had made an unholy mistake. Of course, there was no way now of knowing for sure one way or the other if Trevor was in fact correct, that is until if and when the bush grew back and indeed whether or not any butterflies returned. Either way he was starting to feel too weary from all the aggravation and the effects of his whisky to start to delve into the issue. Let time take its course he thought to himself as he reluctantly made his way home.

The passing weeks were easier for Roger as, happily, the incident in the garden no longer seemed to be at the forefront of Sylvia's mind. Life resumed at the pace it had previously been and they both continued with the familiarly that is part and parcel of a long marriage, although with a certain amount of indifference which had surreptitiously crept in between them. Sylvia seemed to spend a lot more time at her coveted beauty salon plus shopping expeditions to Keaton's Department store in town, coming back each time with more additions to her already overflowing wardrobe. Roger continued to frequent the bar at the golf club and, on occasion, played a round with Lionel when he felt up to it.

And as the days grew longer and the weather started to take a turn for the better, the garden swiftly sprung to life from its self-inflicted hibernation. But because there was the absence of Trevor's knowledgeable eyes, the plants and shrubs plus copious amounts of weeds started to behave like naughty children going totally out of control. It was as if they were all getting their own back for the dismissal of their favourite teacher. Directly at the back of the garden the two houses that unexpectedly had been given centre stage a few months before were now once more totally obscured from view. For the space they had once temporarily occupied was now filled by the most glorious bush. It soared up beyond the boundary fence defiantly obstructing anything that might try to commandeer its position. The bush had reawakened and usurped its former glory with a wonderful array of eye-catching, Empire Blue blooms that were now continually attracting cascades of butterflies, just as Trevor Long's parting words had predicted.

'You do realise what you've done, don't you?' said Roger, angrily coming into the kitchen one lunchtime after returning home from meeting Lionel at the club.

'What on earth are you talking about, and don't use that tone to me, Roger,' Sylvia replied as she continued to prepare the gravy.

'Trevor Long, and don't tell me you didn't know,' he answered, raising his voice still further in aggravated anger. Never before had he spoken to Sylvia this way, so the shock was as much to his system as to his wife, whose face spoke volumes.

Oh yes, she knew, and had done for ages.

'Your spiteful words had the desired effect,' Roger continued, 'because no one round here seems to want to employ him again. And as if that wasn't bad enough, the poor man has had a complete breakdown. Apparently according to Lionel he's been in St Vincent's Hospital for the past two weeks.'

Sylvia couldn't reply, knowing only too well she was the culprit.

The following week by way of trying to make some amends to Roger, she joined St Vincent's hospital volunteers and started visiting lonely inpatients, usually taking in some fresh-cut flowers from the garden. She also started to take an interest by reading up and looking after the garden herself by way of an apology to Trevor and, although at first it was unyielding, eventually she managed to make inroads. A drastic change also came about Sylvia herself with visits to the beauty salon suspended, as she had no time for frivolities now with so much to do outside in the open air. She also managed, by way of Roger, to have Trevor's good character restored although whether or not he would ever be able to put it to good use again was another matter. He remained shut away in the psychiatric department with no time limit on his stay. Every Monday, Sylvia would take some freshly cut flowers in and arrange them in a vase, before letting one of the nurses take them to place on Trevor's bedside table. The young nurses always commented on the striking, ever-changing, floral displays, often remarking that it was such a shame that Trevor hardly seemed to register them for, on the rare occasions that he did, he wasn't even able to tell one flower from the other.

ABOUT THE AUTHOR

Marianne Price has been a singer and actress for more than fifty years and has worked in cabaret, television, West End musical theatre, tours, repertory theatre, radio and film. She is also a highly sort after public and after dinner speaker.

Marianne comes from Tottenham, North London, where at the age of fifteen she started out singing in the working men's clubs and pubs in the area and also in the East End. She went on to perform leading roles in various musicals as a member of Joan Littlewood's Theatre Workshop at the Theatre Royal Stratford East and as a solo singer in the theatre's Sunday Cabaret nights. She also was a performer in a Royal Variety Performance at the London Palladium. In musical theatre in the West End, Marianne played roles in many well-known shows including 'The Rocky Horror Show', 'Evita' and 'Little Me'. Notable are playing – Sheila in 'Hair' at the Shaftesbury Theatre, 'Jeannie in the revival of 'Hair' at Her Majesty's Theatre, taking over the role of Rita from Elaine Paige in 'Billy' opposite Michael Crawford at the Theatre Royal Drury Lane and performing the role of Sandy in the original London production of 'Grease' at the New London Theatre opposite Richard Gere.

Over twenty-five years ago when living in an old house overlooking the sea in Suffolk, she started writing short stories and also poetry. She has won poetry competitions and her work has also been published.

Marianne now lives in Southport on the coast in the North West of England with her husband where she recently performed the role of Norma Desmond in ‘Sunset Boulevard’ at the Little Theatre.

She can be contacted at marianneprice@envance.co.uk

Printed in Great Britain
by Amazon